Mall Hair Maladies

KRISTY JO VOLCHKO

MALL HAIR MALADIES
Copyright © 2017 by Kristy Jo Volchko

Cackleberry Creek Publishing LLC
Pittsburgh, Pennsylvania
CackleberryCkPublishing@gmail.com

For more information or to book an event, please contact:
KristyJoVolchko@gmail.com
CackleberryCkPublishing@gmail.com
www.kristyjovolchko.com
@KristyJoVolchko
@CackleberryBks

ISBN 978-0692972748
ISBN 0692972749

Edited by Eve Arroyo Editing - evearroyo.com
and Kat Helgeson - kathelgeson.wordpress.com
Cover Design by Steven Novak - novakillustration.com
Formatted by The Book Khaleesi - www.thebookkhaleesi.com

Books by Kristy Jo Volchko

Frogs Can Fly

There Are No Monsters at Cackleberry Creek!

The Clubhouse Cabobble

Operation Scrub-A-Dub Skunk

Mall Hair Maladies

For every 80s kid

~ * ~

Spring 1986

*T*here are some who might think that fourteen years on the Earth isn't long enough to know a thing or two about life, but I do. I mean, just in the last year alone I've learned a *ton* of valuable lessons and pondered some of life's greatest mysteries. For example, why don't nails ever dry as fast you need them to? I wonder, as I sit on the edge of my bed, wiggling my fingers in front of my mini fan. *Cool Cascade,* the bottle says, but why don't they just call it what it is, light pink? And who are *they,* exactly?

"Tanya, fifteen minutes!" My mom calls up the stairs.

My stomach flutters with excitement. "Kay."

I smile to myself and think about fate. Destiny. Serendipity. Good ol' fashioned luck. It's not something

I'd given much thought to until recently. Not everyone believes in fate, you know, but I've learned that all it takes is one chance meeting or moment to change everything.

It's not like I'm a super dramatic kind of chick either. I mean, some of my friends are like, totally histrionic, so when I tell you that one single day changed my entire life—jolted it like the first time you dared to stick your tongue to a 9-volt battery—it's just a fact. You don't always see fate coming. I know I didn't.

I glance at the boxes stacked in the corner of my soon-to-be-old bedroom and regret not packing the poster collages I should've taken down days ago. I worked on those for months. I still haven't decided what to do with my *so last year* fluorescent belts dangling from the closet hook, or the 124 color-coordinated jelly bracelets that now decorate the arms and legs of my Raggedy Ann doll. I can't believe I ever wore those, what a phase. Still, I'd rather leave them here and wonder what became of them instead of tossing them in the garbage and witnessing two years of my allowance go down the drain. Maybe the realtor could pass them on to a daughter or niece or something. I thought about pitching them into one of the boxes in the garage that has "Salv-Army Donations" scrawled across the flaps, but I have a hard time picturing some homeless person or little old lady walking the streets sporting my spiked bracelets and hot pink jelly shoes.

MALL HAIR MALADIES

The shoes (torture devices) I wore only once, for about an hour, and ended up walking home barefoot from St. Luke's carnival because my feet were screaming in pain. Within five blocks blisters had already formed, and there were little X shaped indents where they had mercilessly dug into my skin. Obviously, whoever invented those rubber catastrophes never took more than three steps in them.

Since this stupid fan is useless, I blow and blow on my nails until I'm dizzy and think about how completely different my life was a year ago. Looking back, I see things click perfectly into place like some bizarre fate puzzle I didn't even know I was a part of at the time. But now that I'm fourteen I'm a lot smarter about these things.

I hold my breath, spray my hair a full seven seconds, and slide my nyloned feet into new, white pumps. Grown-up shoes.

Suddenly, I'm overwhelmed with a flood of emotion. I swallow down the lump in my throat and will myself not to cry, knowing there's no time to redo my makeup if the tears come. *Think of happy ABCs, Tanya. Apple pie, angels, butterflies, bunny rabbits, boy bands, Christmas, cupcakes...*

It seems like only yesterday I hid inside this closet, sobbing hysterically on the first day of kindergarten because I wasn't allowed to wear Wonder Woman Underoos as a legitimate school outfit. And that's when it hits me; I'm seriously going to miss these lilac-painted, poster-covered walls with the glow in the dark ceiling stickers and chipped baseboards.

This room is where I played with dolls, painted by numbers, left teeth for the tooth fairy, and cookies for Santa, scribbled valentines, decorated aluminum foil shoe boxes with construction paper hearts, sang along to countless records, experimented with makeup, and referred to myself as "Sandy" from the movie *Grease* for two months straight. How many times had I danced in front of this antique, silver mirror as I tried on my mom's bras, just to see what it felt like to wear one? (I think I was pretending to be Marilyn when I stuffed in the socks.)

I thought of my tenth birthday sleepover when my friends and I were jumping on the bed to the song "Super Freak" and split the headboard in half. We spent the rest of the evening trying to fix it, first with craft glue and tied together shoe strings, then black electrical tape I'd found in the garage. I ended up just draping a few afghans over it and calling it a night. I successfully hid the damage for about a week until I came home from school to find the headboard gone and my mom waiting to have a talk about communication and honesty.

This headboard-less bed had heard years of mumbled goodnight prayers and countless tales about little piggies, pokey puppies, Arabian nights, magic carpets, magnificent castles with handsome princes, and wicked stepmothers bearing poison fruit.

MALL HAIR MALADIES

My mother had tucked me in with a story every single night until I announced (at the tender age of eight) that I was *not* a baby anymore and too old for such things. A few days later she "slept" in the hard desk chair next to my bed holding a puke bucket and placing cool rags on my forehead when I had the stomach flu. I cried all night, not because I was throwing up, but because I was too sick to go trick or treating, and it only came once a year.

I stare out the window at the tiny buds sprouting from the tree branches and Mrs. Dezak's poodle pooping next to her mailbox (gross) and realize I'll never again look out this window and see the day's end orange-pink horizon, or the first snowfall of the season blanketing the neighborhood.

I hope whoever moves in next will be just as happy here. Will it be a grown-up or a kid? A girl my age, or a cute Matt Dillon look-alike? Perhaps it'll be a nursery for some sweet, little baby. I wonder if they'll even notice the family of cardinals that builds a nest outside my window between the roof and the gutter each spring.

My stomach flip-flops with a mixture of sadness, happiness, and excitement all at the same time. But change is inevitable, right? I mean, we can't all stay in our childhood rooms until we're old and grey, writing letters to Santa, lying upside down on a bed doodling on an Etch-A-Sketch, and inserting multi-colored, vacuum unfriendly pegs into a Lite-Brite toy.

I take a deep breath and let it out slowly, just like the soothing voice from my mom's yoga tape says. Welp, onward and upward, out with the old, in with the new, and all that wise stuff. This is a day to celebrate! *Goodbye forever, room. You're the best one a girl could have ever asked for.* I blow my room one last kiss. It's go time!

New Kid on the Block

One year earlier...

here's just something about spring that gets me really wound up. It's like I don't even realize how cooped up I've felt until the first hint of warm weather appears, or when some annoying bird peeps me awake on a Sunday morning. Then I know spring is officially here and I want to run, run, run! Don't get me wrong, cold, snowy weather can be cool for building snowmen, sledding, and snowball blasting—just not when you walk to and from school every day, and it lasts for six and a half months!

Around April Fools' Day, spring fever had hit my class with a vengeance. We had about nine weeks left of eighth grade and then, bye-bye Seaton Junior High!

(Go Cougars!) Wasn't there some kind of quote that says life doesn't really begin until high school? Anyway, as the weather grew warmer, the hallways got crazier, the principal's office filled with busted class cutters, and teachers and students alike seemed to be in a daze as they stared longingly out of the now opened windows that teased us with a breeze—tormenting those who longed to be outdoors. Everyone was so ready for Easter break.

Even though I had a lot going on with final exams, graduation, yearbook committee, and choosing that year's summer camp package (I was torn between Center Arts Camp or Softball Camp) I had only *one* thing on my mind—the upcoming Madonna concert.

The universal pop gods had bestowed upon my city the gift of an official tour date. The queen of pop music, the one and only goddess of girls, young and old, was coming to Pittsburgh in May! In fact, that's how Randi and I became instant best friends, our mutual obsession with all things Madonna.

Randi had just moved here from New York and had the sass to prove it. It was the first day back from Thanksgiving break, and I was in the school office (the zoo) dropping off yearbook photos from the Harvest Dance. Our principal, Mrs. Miller, hurried from her doom-room with a girl my age wearing a jean jacket and a T-shirt that said "Relax" on it. She had wildly-teased, jet-black hair, wore about a hundred bracelets all the way up both arms, and chawed her gum with brutal force.

Mrs. Miller practically shoved her at me, "Tanya, I'd like to introduce you to our new student, Randi Gattano."

I smiled politely and shook her sticky hand.

"Dear, would you mind showing Randi around school today? I think you share some of the same courses." She scribbled two hall passes for us. "Show her around, but don't dilly dally."

Me? Dilly dally?

We both looked down at Mrs. Miller's big toe sticking out from the gigantic hole in her pantyhose and grinned at each other. *Good, she has a sense of humor.*

I stuffed down my urge to laugh. "Uh, yeah, sure."

But Mrs. Miller had already shut her door.

Once we were out in the hall we burst into giggles. "That was one whopper of a hole!" I hooted. "I guess open toe shoes *really* means open toe shoes!"

Randi laughed. "Yeah, there's nooo way clear nail polish is gonna fix that runner!"

She rummaged through her denim tote, which had a bunch of "I Love NY" and "Bugle Boy" buttons pinned across the strap and retrieved two pieces of watermelon bubble gum. She handed one to me, spit her old one into a wad of tissue while unwrapping another, all in one fell swoop. She smiled. "Time for a new piece."

"Thanks," I said, biting off half of mine and pocketing the rest for later. "Watermelon's my number one fav flav."

"Oh, yeah? Me too."

I thought she talked funny. The way she pronounced yeah sounded like *yee-ah*, and the word too like toe (as in big toe, pinky toe, Mrs. Miller's toe). It had attitude. I liked it.

She snapped a huge bubble and said, "I heard it's Madonna's favorite too. That, and unbuttered popcorn and apple lollies, according to the articles."

I stopped in my tracks. Was this chick for real?

"Whaa? What'd I say?"

"I absolutely *love* her, that's what. Ask me anything. I seriously know everything there is to know."

She thought for a moment. "All right, okay, what's her favorite hairspray?"

I chuckled, "Well, maybe not that *one* thing."

She opened up her Trapper Keeper. "Check this out."

I stared in awe at the array of photo clips and bubble stickers that decorated her entire binder front to back. "Where'd you get all these?"

I considered myself the ultimate Madonna collector and hadn't seen *half* of them. I used my weekly allowance of $5.75 to buy posters and magazines that held only her best photos, posters, and articles. Well, that and hairspray, tapes, and jelly bracelets. You know, the real necessities.

Randi said, "My pen pal from Arizona sends some good ones. I found her name in the back of *Bop Maga-*

zine."

"Yeah, I've seen those," I said. "They're under that Pen Pal Connection ad."

Randi nodded, "Yep. And my uncle Tony says he thought he saw Madonna hanging up flyers for a gig once, right outside his pizzeria, like, right before she got famous. I guess she doesn't need to do that anymore."

"Wow!" It felt cool to know someone, who knows someone, who saw her in person before! I was fascinated by this new girl and her impressive trapper keeper, dazzling accessories, big, crimped-out hair, and silver, hoop earrings. I had to know more.

I blasted her with questions. "So, Gattano... what's that? Italian? Randi... after your dad, right? Do you like Pittsburgh so far? I'm sorry, I'm asking a million questions, just tell me to shut up."

She unwrapped her third piece of gum and laughed at my crazy energy. "It's okay. At least you're not boring, right?"

I hadn't thought of it that way. Sometimes my brain ran a mile a minute about a thousand things at once. I suppose that was better than having no thoughts at all.

Randi looked at one of her Swatch watches. "I'm not keeping you from class, am I?"

"Oh, no, I'm supposed to be at gym right now, then lunch. Plus, we've got these." I held up my pass with the unreadable writing. Chicken scratch, I called it.

"Okay, good. So, Randi... named after my grandpa Rodolpho. I think they were expecting a boy, so I ended up with Randi. Thank gawd I dodged a bullet there, eh? I mean, Rodolpho?" She pointed down her throat, "Gag!"

I laughed. "I like Randi. It's different, it suits you."

"Thanks. So, yeah, Gattano's Italian. I'm originally from New Jersey, but my mom wanted to try acting so we moved to New York. Now it's just me and my dad, they... they're divorced. It's a boring story, but basically, she wanted to focus more on her career and lives out in LA now. So far, she's appeared as a hostess at a car convention, had her picture in a greeting card calendar, and is in that one commercial... the one where those ladies are dancing around with those triple action sponge mops. You ever see it?"

I shook my head.

"Well, my mom's the one with the yellow skirt." She shrugged. "I used to ask my dad why she never visits, but he just said, "Artists are complicated.""

I thought about how sad I'd feel if I hardly saw my mom. I couldn't imagine it.

Randi saw the look on my face and said, "I'm pretty close with my aunts, uncles, and cousins though. And believe me, having *my* aunts is like having *ten* moms!" She smeared on some mint scented lip balm and rubbed her lips together. "Anyway, our family runs a few pizzerias in the city, and when my *nonno* passed away a few months back, my dad decided to sell ours and open up a nursery. He said he's tired of pizza, tired of the scenery. So here we are. It's cool, but I miss my friends."

"A nursery? He takes care of babies?"

She laughed, "Nooo! Like plants and trees."

"Oh, a garden store. That's nice."

When we got to the second-floor gym, I peeked in the door and saw my class picking teams for volleyball.

"So, this is the gym," I said, loud enough for Mrs. Miller to hear as she breezed by without looking our way. "What's your locker number?"

She pulled out a small card from her jacket pocket. "Um... 211."

"You're, like, two down from me!"

Randi smiled, "I guess it's fate."

"Yeah." I nodded. "Fate."

We wandered around the rest of the morning (dilly dallied) as we played twenty questions, loafed in the bathroom, and decorated her new locker. I introduced her to the girls from the yearbook committee, and my closest friends, Stacy Cavanaugh and Paula Pratt. Those two were next door neighbors, best friends, and so close that sometimes, I had to admit, I felt a bit left out.

Randi was an instant hit. "The New York girl," they called her. She had rad clothes, a wicked accent, and by far *the* best hair out of everyone in the school. And from that day on, we were inseparable.

Mall Hair Extraordinaire

Read the back of the can, Tanya."

"I know how to use hairspray, *Mom*."

"Apparently not, you're using half the can!" She waved her hands dramatically in front of her face and opened the hall window. "I can taste the stuff in my mouth for an hour after you're through. A few sprays will do the trick, I'm sure."

I grabbed the can and read aloud to prove a point. "Directions: Shake can before use. Keep can upright ten to twelve inches from hair and spray evenly. Replace cap after use. See? It doesn't say how much to use or not use."

Mom opened the bathroom window. "I suggest you read further down at the list of warnings and the amount of chemicals you're spraying into the environment."

"Thanks for the hairspray 101, Mom, but I'm good. Besides, it's my human right to have hard hair."

Mom raised her eyebrows at me. "I think you're confused about what human rights are exactly."

Personally, I thought she was bonkers to suggest I leave the house without my hair stiffened properly. A single gust of wind could destroy the feathered masterpiece I'd slaved a half an hour for. Did she think great hair just grew out of your head?

But my mom is an environmental attorney and takes this stuff *very* seriously. At any random moment I could a catch a speech on what chemicals were used for this or that and the environmental impact they had. She used nothing but shampoo on her own waist-length, chestnut hair, which got real wavy when it rained. I told her if she put some mousse or gel in it or something it wouldn't get so frizzy, but she doesn't listen.

She wore little to no makeup and preferred bare feet or flip-flops when she wasn't at the office. I thought she was pretty for being an ex-hippie though. Every so often, I'd remind her that if she got a little dolled up and didn't spend so much time at the library organizing some cause, she'd have tons of boyfriends ringing her phone off the hook. But she just laughs and says, "Oh, Tanya. I'm very happy with my life."

I wasn't so sure.

No matter how busy things were she always made

time for the two of us to go shopping or to a movie, work in the garden or do crafts. My absolute favorite was going to the craft store. She let me pick out any colored beads and yarn I wanted, and we'd spend the afternoon nibbling on a fruit and veggie tray, making dream catchers, wind chimes, and mandalas, which she hung on the sunporch or gave away as gifts. I knew none of my friends liked hanging out with their moms, but, somehow, mine could make even doing chores a blast.

On Saturdays she drove almost an hour to Moore's Farm for fresh eggs, goat cheese, and organic fruits and veggies. Why she didn't just drive five minutes down the road to Food-Lot and grab tacos and pop was beyond me. It'd be so much easier.

I had to admit, for being total opposites, we got along extraordinarily well, only having issues when it came to my school work, health, or safety. And she considered my over usage of hair products, and generous consumption of gummy bears an issue.

I heard the phone ring then Mom laughing. It must be Aunt Trish. She wasn't really my aunt, but they'd been best friends since they were girls, so that's what I'd always called her.

Tonight, they were headed to some kind of whale preservation meeting. Piles of "Save the Whales" flyers had littered our dining room table all week. Save them from what? Was there some kind of sicky out there who hated them? There weren't even any whales in the rivers of Pittsburgh, and we had three of them. There might be alligators, piranhas, and secret river monsters, but I knew for sure there were no whales.

"Mom, Randi's gonna call when she's on her way... please don't tie up the phone line," I begged, as I put the finishing touches on my precisely lined, glittered lips.

She appeared in my doorway wearing a dark brown turtleneck with two strands of beads and tan corduroys. We were really going to have to discuss her wardrobe.

"Honey, have you seen my pocketbook?" she asked.

"You mean your purse? It's on the kitchen stool." If it's not a book that fits in your pocket, why did people call it a pocketbook? One of life's many mysteries, I guess.

"I swear I was just in there." She walked out mumbling, "blind as a bat."

She was back in just a moment handing me $6.00 for allowance. (Nice, a quarter raise!) "Are you sure you don't need a ride?"

I spritzed myself with Vanilla Musk. "Thanks, but Randi's dad is dropping us off, remember? Next week it's your turn." I gave her one of my best smiles and sang, "I love yooou."

"Love you too, honey, and make sure you're home by 10:30."

"Yes, Jacqueline."

KRISTY JO VOLCHKO

She gave me a funny look and air kissed me good-bye. I watched her walk down the driveway and climb into Aunt Trish's silver punch buggy. Now I could finish my hair without the hairspray police breathing down my neck, monitoring my usage by the ounce. Superior hair took real effort, concentration, and, most of all, an ample supply of product. No one ever got this kind of bodacious 'do by being lazy and using just one squirt of spray. No, siree, there was a whole science to it. I even had my own ten-step process that I was more than happy to share with anyone who asked (mostly fifth graders). It was my firm belief that no one should miss out on rockin' hair!

1. First, wash the crap out from yesterday because if you don't, you'll have a bunch of gross, white product buildup, and people might think you have lice or something.

2. Towel dry and immediately apply a small amount of mousse or gel (or both) all through it. Plug your style irons in so they'll be plenty hot enough after your blow dry.

3. Blow dry/tousle *upside down* for maximum volume and curls.

4. When dry, spray a round of hairspray while your head is *still* upside down, and begin using

a pick to tease the back, sides, and roots out as much as possible.

5. Flip hair upright, (ignore the dizziness, it goes away) and curl bangs upward, teasing to maximum height. You may also style them to the side, or under (your choice). Crimp the sides, tease, then spray once more until desired hardness. (You're almost done.)

6. Hold a handheld mirror up to view the back of your head in another larger mirror and use a pick to fluff up any flat areas.

7. Re-spray back.

8. Select plain looking pieces throughout and add curl or crimp. Spray entire head for a minimum seven-second count.

9. Allow hair to set while you do your makeup.

10. Before unplugging your irons, apply finishing touches on danger areas — places that could possibly fall flat or lose curl. Spray once more and be prepared to receive a *ton* of compliments on your gorgeously wild, rocked-out hair!

Randi's horn beeped out front. I grabbed my beloved

can of Aqua Net Unscented, Super Hold, teased my light blonde hair out another four inches, and re-sprayed it stiff as a brick. Voila! Mall hair extraordinaire.

~ * ~

Randi and I sat in the corner booth of the food court entrance counting our money. *The* best spot to be to see who was arriving. We loved checking out the high school kids, what outfits they wore, how they did their hair. We called it fashion research.

Randi sopped up the last bit of cheese with her soft pretzel. "This mall is jammed tonight. What shops ya wanna hit first?"

"Parkville Center's always packed," I said, licking the pizza sauce off my greasy fingers. Why didn't I just get a pretzel? "I wanna stop at Revco for light blue polish, you know, for Spring. I'm painting each nail a different pastel. I have eighteen bottles in my collection so far," I announced proudly.

"Ooh, blue, I like that!" Randi inspected her own chipped nails and made a face. "I let mine go all week, not even a top coat. I might alternate silver, gold, silver, gold."

"A futuristic vibe. Nice!"

We were doing what we did every Friday night, malling it up. We'd crash at my house on Friday and hers on Saturday. Paula and Stacy usually met us at the food court around 7-ish, then we'd snack, shop, and boogie down to the first-floor arcade where all the coolest cats hung out.

Lately, it was impossible to get on a game, though. Lots of kids had "Pac-Man Fever" and were lined up for hours sometimes. Last week we barely squeezed through the door because of that new *Terminato-X* game.

We referred to the more serious gamers as, zombie space invaders because everywhere you turned, there they were taking up space with their plastic cups full of quarters, wandering from game to game with that dazed, zombie look in their eyes. Once in a while, we'd get lucky and snag an available pinball machine and play doubles.

Without a doubt, Parkville Arcadia was the soul and heartbeat of the mall, and I could see why kids from all over the 'Burgh' preferred this arcade over all others. Along with the basic games like *Donkey Kong*, *Pac-Man*, *Asteroids*, and *Missile Command*, there were pool tables and rows of Skee-Ball, air hockey, foosball, and bowling machines.

Large speakers hung from the ceiling, pumping out the latest in alternative rock, and there was a roped off area where people could dance under multicolored strobe lights. The four of us danced *only* when a tubular tune came on and we simply *had* to. It was also where they had relocated all the photo booths. The four of us would cram into one and spend a small fortune making silly faces and hamming it up, just to wait twenty minutes for the slot to puke out a blurry strip of smudged photos. I already had dozens tacked up on my bedroom bulletin board.

"The girls should've been here by now," I said. "I hope they didn't start shopping without us."

Randi slurped her root beer Slushie and let out a tiny burp. "Paula said Stacy's grounded this weekend. You know she won't come without her."

I rolled my eyes. "That girl's *always* in trouble."

Just then, I spotted Jay Garrick at the counter of Chili-Dog-Dare-Ya. His family owned Garrick's Market down the block from my house and, in my opinion, had the best variety of ice cream and penny candy around.

All I really knew about him was that he was fifteen and in the tenth grade, liked to chew Big League gum, and had played baseball since he could walk. There were a ton of pictures on the wall behind the cash register of him wearing different uniforms throughout the years. My favorite was the one of him standing next to a real Pittsburgh Pirate, but the autograph across the bottom was all smudged so I couldn't tell which one.

I made it a point never to go in on Wednesday or Sunday afternoons when he stocked shelves. I just knew I'd do something stupid like trip and fall. Or worse, what if he had to ring up my order, and I sneezed and couldn't get a tissue in time? Then he'd think of me as "booger girl" forever. I was also afraid that if I had to hand him money my hand would shake from adrenaline, and he'd think I was a total creepoid. No, it was much safer to go in when his sister Robin was working. I heard she recently received a basketball scholarship to some bangin' university this fall. I could see why, too, she was literally the tallest girl I'd ever seen. Maybe on Earth.

I dug frantically through my purse for a compact but all I got was a fistful of blue eyeshadow that had cracked out of its container and spilled. Cripes! I must've left it on the bed. I grinned at Randi like a demented clown. "Quick, do I have sauce in my teeth?"

She practically choked on her drink. "No, you're good."

"I knew from my horoscope this morning I'd run into him. It was all, 'Scorpio, with the Sun in Aries your love life is on fire as Mars enters... something, blah, blah.' Anyway, I just knew I'd see him."

Jay looked beyond gorgeous, wearing a navy-blue Seaton High baseball shirt with Garrick written across the back and his dark brown hair spiked to perfection.

I sighed. "He's a total ace."

The two of us rated boys like a poker deck. Most were twos through tens, and here and there we'd spot a jack or king, but Jay was an ace of hearts. Their suit was based on hair color, so if I told Randi I saw a jack of clubs, she'd know that meant a cutie pie with dark hair. A king was breathtaking, an ace perfection. A

spade was a bad-boy type of all hair colors, and a dia-
mond was always blonde. I'd never seen a handsome
redhead, so it didn't matter. But hearts... that suit went
to who you were crazy about—the one who had your
heart.

"Man, I can't *wait* until ninth grade," I said. "Come
September, Jay and I will be strolling the same halls.
Maybe we'll even have the same lunch or independent
study period."

Randi nodded. "That'd be stellar."

I fantasized that one day, I'd be running late to
class and clumsily drop my math book. Suddenly, Jay
would swoop in out of nowhere, catch it midair, and
spin it on the tip of his finger like a basketball. (Impressive!) When he hands it over, our eyes meet, and there
will be instant electricity. Like lightning bolts or when
your socks are fresh out of the dryer and you get those
annoying little static shocks. And I don't turn red or
say anything stupid.

He'll smile charmingly. "Math is very important,
Tanya. You may need this."

"But... how did you know my name?"

He'll say, "Because I love you. You're the most incredible girl in the entire school, the city, the world!"
He'll take my hand. "Make me the happiest guy in the
galaxy. Be my date for the prom?"

How could I say no to that?

We'll spin into a waltz, our moves so fresh it'll look
like we've danced together since kindergarten! We'll

positively glow as a beam of sunlight shines down on us through the window like a spotlight from a Broadway stage. All the kids standing around will clap and spread apart to make room as we twirl and twirl and twirl and twirl...

"Hellooo." Randi waved her hands in front of my glazed eyes. "Earth to Tanya, ooh-we-ooh."

I laughed. "Hey, do you think if we got married, he'd pick Oliver Morris to be his best man? He's cute, right? Naturally, you'd be my maid of honor, and yinz would look so sweet together... awww."

Randi scrunched up her face. *"Non c`e` modo!"* (No way!) I loved when she reacted in Italian. "At best he's a seven of clubs. But *Oliver?"* She shook her head. "Sorry, no-can-do. There's no way I can handle that grandpa name he's got. I'd probably end up just calling him *dude* or renaming him altogether. I'll bet his middle name is even dorkier, like Harold or Rufus. No, wait... Stanley or Burt."

I was laughing so hard I could barely speak. "No way, it's gotta be Arthur or Fred."

She said, "You're way off, I'd bet my right, pinky toenail it's Barney or Maximillian!"

I held my stomach and gasped for air. "I can picture it now. Do you, Randi Gattano, take Oliver Harold Eugene Morris III to be your lawfully wedded husband?"

We were howling. I had no idea why I found it so hysterical.

A tear streamed down Randi's cheek. "Stop! You're ruining my mascara!" She tried to catch her breath as she dabbed at her makeup. "First, Miss Wedding Planner, you should probably start by saying hello."

I blew my nose, which always seemed to run when I laughed really hard. "Yeah, yeah. One of these days when I'm buying penny candy I'll ask his professional opinion on the Wacky Taffy." I threw my wad of napkins in the garbage, never taking my eyes off Jay. He was smiling at something Oliver (dude) was saying.

Randi threaded her arm through mine so I wouldn't trip over my own feet. "Are you ready to shop?"

I bravely blew a kiss his way. "Totally."

Bubble Dreams

*L*ater that night, Randi and I sprawled out on my bedroom floor doing our nails, trading jelly bracelets, and cutting magazine clips for the wall collage we'd been working on for the last two months. "Little Red Corvette" was just finishing from our number one favorite station on the planet, B-94, when we heard, "This is Adam O'Maraaaa at the Bee, announcing your chance to see Madonnnnna live! Yes, live! When you hear any Madonna intro tonight, just be caller number ten and we'll see you, *and* a friend, May 28th at the Civic Arenaaahh! Stop by your local National Record Mart for tickets, but hurry... they're selling out fast! Listen all weekend long for chances to win tour shirts, posters, cassette packs, backstage passes, and more! 555-9494. Don't miss your chance to rock the night away in style!"

I jerked up so fast my bowl of corn chips flew everywhere. "Backstage passes!"

"Tanya!" Randi plucked chips from her lap and hair.

I grabbed my hamburger phone, set it between us, and pre-dialed to it B-94 so I'd only have to press redial when the time came. I was actually trembling.

If I won free tickets, my mom would be less inclined to say no to my going. After all, the concert was on a Tuesday night—a school night, and I got the feeling that my mom wasn't too fond of my newest pop crush. She didn't come right out and say it exactly, but I could tell by the way she scrunched up her face for a microsecond when I mentioned her, like she'd just taken a whiff of outdated milk or lunch meat.

At that moment, I had about seventy-five cents to my name and this was the first I was hearing of an actual tour date. The magazines had said to watch for a *possible* summer tour. This was early spring! Had I known just a day earlier, I wouldn't have blown all my dough on blue nail polish, two cans of hairspray, a can of mousse, blue eyeliner with matching mascara, a six-pack of jelly bracelets, food court pizza, the April issue of *Teen Street*, and a pack of glittered, butterfly stickers for my binder. No matter, winning the tickets would be easy, we just had to keep on top of it. In fact, we'd probably have them by the end of the weekend. And if, by some freak stroke of bad luck I didn't win them (unthinkable), my plan B was to approach it with my mom like an early birthday present. Sure, my birthday wasn't until early November, seven months away, but birthdays were always good negotiating tools, and certainly worth a try.

My mind raced as I played out all the possible ticket possession scenarios in my head. "Okay, I'm gonna use the bathroom so I don't miss any announcements," I said. "If you hear even *one* intro bar, you know what to do."

She rolled onto her stomach, stripped the plastic off a Fruit Roll-Up,' and opened her magazine. "Gotcha."

I dashed to and from the bathroom as fast as humanly possible, somersaulted across my bed, and turned the radio up. I was really wound up!

Randi giggled. "You're seriously bonkers." She shook her head at a two-page spread of Cyndi Lauper. "I swear, every shot I see of her lately she's got her mouth wide open. Does she just go through every shoot like, ahh, yah, haaa? And that fashion, I can't get into it, man. It's like, she throws on a bunch of stuff, and the gimmick is, 'I'm totally unusual because I'm wearing a tutu with a million necklaces and a checkered shirt.'" She slid the magazine over to me. "And that shaved head? Forget about it."

I took a quick look. "Yeah, I liked her better before she shaved the side of her head into a checkerboard design."

Randi asked, "If you could ask Madonna one question, what would it be?"

"Just one? Besides, pretty please, please, please can I touch one of your laced gloves or your hair? Go on tour with you and be your assistant?" I laughed. "No, I'd either ask her how it feels to be a huge mega-star or how does she dance on stage in those high heels without ever falling off. One of those triple spins of hers and I'd be on the floor with a broken shinbone! Seriously, how does she do it?"

Randi said, "A *ton* of hard work and practice, I'm sure. I'd ask her if she ever got nervous before going on stage. She's just so... fearless. It takes real courage to sing and dance and talk in front of the world like that. And she does those TV interviews like it's no big whoop. And those jealous people are always saying crappy stuff about her... but she raises her chin even higher and blows 'em off like, this is who I am, like it or not. That's some *seriously* thick skin!"

I said, "That's why she's the queen!" I knew what she meant though. Many times, I'd wished I had that kind of pizzazz. And when one of her songs came on it made me feel... I don't know... confident, expressive, even glamorous. I loved everything about her—music, fashion, attitude—and I knew when I grew up, I wanted to be *just* like her. Not topping the charts necessarily, but edgy and bold, knowing what I wanted and going after it all the way. I loved reading the articles where she talked about how she never gave up on her dreams, even when times were tough, and didn't let the naysayers get in her head. She believed in herself, and her determination was inspiring. Sometimes, when I had the house to myself, I'd crank up the music, close my eyes, dance, sing, and pretend I *was* her! If anyone ever saw me, I'd die of embarrassment!

Randi glued a *Purple Rain* clip onto the collage between Joan Jett and Duran Duran and said, "I read somewhere that some of these pop artists get their jewelry and clothing from thrift shops then cut up the tees, make fingerless gloves, skirts, and leggings—you know, *their* style and vision."

"Sounds easy enough," I said. "Think of all the outfits we could make if we put our minds to it." I studied a clip of Madonna, dressed in black with spiked bracelets up both arms. This was the shot that made me change the way I did my eyeliner and start crimping out my hair. Her accessories definitely looked original to me. I looked closer, was she using pantyhose as hair ties?

"I have an idea," I said, jumping up and sock skiing down the hallway, hardwood floor. I yelled downstairs to my mom, who was in the dining room with Aunt Trish. "Ma, can I have your old nylons with the runs in them?"

"What? Why?"

"I'm making something."

"Uh... sure."

"And can I borrow some of Aunt Marge's old costume jewelry?"

"Yes, but just the stuff from the hat box."

"Thank you!"

I went to her room and fished a few pairs of pantyhose from the wastebasket beside the dresser. There were so many! Did the woman go through a pair a day? I slid open her mirrored closet doors and looked specifically for the blue and white floral box that held the clunky jewelry Aunt Marge had given her before moving to a retirement community. Why didn't they just call it what it was, an old people's building? The box smelled like baby powder and mothballs. I used to turn my nose up at this old, crappy stuff, but now... it was 1985 and these things were back in style with a vengeance.

I brought the mothball-smelling, pirate treasure chest of jewels back to my room and dumped the goods on the bed. "Ta da!" I handed Randi the bundle of stockings. "There's navy, there's black, there's cream, there's nude. Why spend the money at Murphy's when we can make our own hair bows and fingerless gloves right here?"

Randi scooped up a fistful of jewelry. "This is fantastic!"

We spent the next hour cutting the legs off pantyhose and turning them into fingerless gloves and hair ties, beading bracelets, necklaces, and anklets into different styles. We attached crucifixes to braided nylons then matched them with colored stones, and strands of faux pearls, ultimately creating head turning, fabulously swanky belts.

Randi twirled in front of the mirror, put her hands on her hips, and did a runway strut across the room. "Tres chic, unique, mystique, for your boutique, dawwling!"

I clapped my hands. "You look sensational! I'm telling you, you've got a real talent for this stuff."

"Thanks. I'm totally gonna be a fashion designer one day. As soon as I graduate I'm headed straight to New York for design school."

That sounded awesome. "Randi, with your looks and talent, you could be both model *and* designer!"

"If only..." she said, laying her designs across the bed. She studied them intensely as if she was about to dress twelve models for a fashion show.

I thought she had a great chance, too. Besides being the prettiest girl in our school, she was always doodling pictures of gowns, dresses, and funky outfits on a giant sketch pad, which she carried under her arm everywhere. She went through colored pencils like crazy.

I said, "Since I'm going to be a photographer I can do the fashion shoots when your collections are ready."

From the time I'd received my first Polaroid camera from Santa I'd been in love with photography. I already had five full albums of everything from birds, to sunsets, random people, school friends, buildings, holiday parties, and even half-eaten pieces of toast I'd nibbled into the shape of a heart. Nothing was off limits. My newest pal, my Kodak 35mm camera, was always in my purse in case a good shot presented itself, or when I was simply in the mood for a shoot. I especially loved the unposed blooper shots of my mom holding her nose while taking out the trash, or with her face contorted mid-sneeze. The ones where Randi's yawning or blowing her nose were pretty funny too, but for some reason I was the only one who thought so.

One time I was on the porch preparing to take shots of honey bees gathering nectar for a science project and, instead, ended up with pictures of our mailman's face as he ran from Goober, my neighbor's poodle. He tripped over a crack in the cement and screamed like a little girl as mail flew everywhere. I knew I shouldn't have been snapping pictures of that scene but how could I not? Those were the *real* moments in life to capture!

I dreamed that one day I'd travel to Paris or London, taking pictures of all the latest fashion, historical architecture, and interesting people. Maybe I'd get a super-fab assignment to some exotic land, capturing rare moments in the lives of gorillas and kangaroos for *National Geographic* or *Time* magazine!

Randi said, "We can both move to New York. We'll live in some chic, little Soho apartment and see all the Broadway musicals and fashion shows."

"Fashion Week!" I screeched! "We'll have our own

company complete with your latest designs, my photography equipment, models, the whole shebang! All the magazines will call *us* for their photo shoots and fashion needs. Watch out, New York, here we come!"

Randi threw her hands in the air. "I love it!"

I reached over and cranked the volume all the way up, and we danced around like maniacs to "99 Red Balloons." We must've sounded like a herd of buffalo coming through the ceiling because my mom yelled, "Girls! Keep it down up there!"

I turned the volume halfway down and called back, "It's our human right to daaaance! Or is this house like that one town where dancing is against the law?" I spun in circles, swinging my head and hair around wildly, like that chick in *Flashdance.* I looked like I was on fire before some random bystander yells, "stop, drop, and roll! Stop, drop, and roll!" Randi was doubled over laughing so hard, no sound came out, and the veins were popping out of her neck and forehead. I could always send her into hysterics.

Suddenly, the intro to "Lucky Star" came on. Oh! Oh! I dove to the floor and grabbed the phone. "This is it; we have to be caller ten!"

I jabbed the redial button, my heartbeat pounding in my ears. *Breathe in through the nose, out through the mouth. "Shheee."*

Neep neep neep, busy signal. Redial. *Neep neep neep.* Over and over I hung up, pressed redial, hung up, pressed redial. Randi knelt beside me on the floor, gnawing her freshly painted nails. I lightly swatted them out of her mouth. Halfway through the song I began to worry that time was running out when... "It's ringing! Oh, please, please, please."

Randi squealed and crossed her fingers.

My face felt hot, and my heartbeat throbbed in my ears. What if I had high blood pressure like my Uncle Doug and I passed out before the DJ answered? What are you supposed to say when they *do* answer? I panicked as I tried to remember what previous winners had said, but mostly they just screamed. I counted five rings before a guy picked up and boomed enthusiastically, "You're caller eight!" *Click.* He hung up!

"Nooooo!" I fumbled with the receiver, my fingers moving like molasses. Redial! Redial! But the line was busy again, and if I was caller eight, they most likely had their number ten by now.

Moments later, my room was filled with the high-pitched yelps of some ticket winning girl. I was actually happy for Maggie, from South Side. I knew if it were me I'd be screaming too. I might've even thrown up on my purple bedspread. In fact, I was feeling kind of nauseated.

Randi hugged me. "It's okay, Tanya-toon. We'll win 'em at my house tomorrow, guaranteed. And if we don't, the concert's still a few weeks away, we'll just buy 'em." She put her hands on my shoulders and looked me in the eyes. "Tanya, we *are* going to that concert."

I nodded. "You're right. I just hope Jackie says I can go."

We traipsed down to the kitchen for a before-bed bowl of cereal. I was beat. Mom and Aunt Trish were in the dining room sifting through boxes of old memorabilia, having a glass of wine, and listening to a Joni Mitchell record. A platter of different colored cheeses sat between them, making the whole room smell like farts. I hated cheese. It wasn't bad on nachos but not in chunks like that.

Aunt Trish is a flight attendant and always brought over weird looking cheeses and bottles of wine from her travels. Through the years she's brought me a variety of collectible dolls from nearly every country, but they're not in my room. Mom puts them in special mothproof bins in the attic for safekeeping. She says they're very valuable, and one day I'll want to pass them down. To whom? I planned on traveling the world one day and I wasn't lugging a bunch of brats around when I did.

My mom thinks Aunt Trish is brilliant. Maybe she is. I know she has a master's degree in... something, I can't remember, and is fluent in several languages. She even wrote a book series called, *Vins Fins de la Decennie, Volumes One & Two*, which translates to, Fine Wines of the Decade. A few times a month the two of them hung out and did something they considered fun; art shows, book signings, theatre events, and sometimes concerts when one of their bands from the olden days came to town. Maybe that'd be me and Randi when we got old.

When Mom spotted us she pointed to a crystal dish full of something that resembled dog poo that's been marinating in someone's yard for a month and asked, "Would you girls like some gourmet crackers and cheese? There's garlic pâte and watercress, too."

Randi smiled politely. "Thanks, Ms. Sheffield, I'm good."

I wrinkled my nose. "You know I hate cheese. It smells like cat puke."

Mom and Aunt Trish looked at each other and burst out laughing.

I didn't see what was so funny.

"Tanya, are those my pantyhose you have tied in your hair?" Mom asked.

I fluffed my crimped-out locks. "Uh-huh."

"And my black hose you're wearing as gloves?"

I put my hands on my hips and posed. "Yep."

Aunt Trish said, "Remember the wild stuff we used to wear, Jackie?"

Mom held up a photo of the two of them at a bonfire. They were wearing layers of beads, rings on every finger, and flowers painted on their faces and across their stomachs. Mom was wearing cutoff jean shorts and a bikini top. Aunt Trish, even less. "How could I forget? Those were groovy times, huh?" She and Aunt Trish exchanged the kind of look that lifelong friends do when they've shared many secrets. The kind I was sure would never reach my ears.

Groovy? This time Randi and I were the ones laughing. They were so weird!

Aunt Trish said to Randi in Italian, *"La tua moda e` favolosa."* (Your fashion looks fabulous.)

Randi smiled, *"Grazie!"*

I gave Mom and Aunt Trish hugs. "Goodnight, you two groooovy chicks."

Aunt Trish said, "Goodnight, totally rad chicks." Then they giggled in a way that made me see what those two must have been like as girls. The way I hoped to always laugh with my best friend.

King of Hearts

The next morning, after Randi took off, I decided to give my room a really good cleaning instead of just jamming everything in my closet and drawers. Things were getting out of hand here. Stuffed animals were coated with dust, my dressing table looked as if a makeup counter had exploded, the mirror had an inch-thick, blurry coating of hairspray across it, and I couldn't even see under my bed anymore.

Mom tapped on my door. I said, "Open sesame."

Suddenly my room was filled with the scent of her citrus oil. She smelled like a tiny orange tree. Her hair, still damp from the shower, hung in a long braid down her back, and she wore a long ankle skirt with butterflies on it, a black tank top, and leather sandals. A real, live hippie chick she was.

"Would you like to come to the farmer's market today? It's gorgeous out."

I didn't even have to think about it. Long car rides with her were torture. Not only did she drive super slow with the windows down, not caring one bit if it destroyed my hair, she refused to put on B-94 FM (bubble-gum pop, she called it). What did she think I thought of her whiny, beat-less, hippy-dippy crapolla? Also, she's been known to randomly pull over and take pictures of clouds she swore were shaped like hearts, rabbits, koalas, or goldfish. The woman could see nature in a bowl of Fruity-Ohs. So, a trip that would take a normal person an hour, to and from, meant half the day for her, and I didn't have that kind of time to waste. I had tickets to win.

"Thanks, mom, but if I stop cleaning now I'll never finish. Plus, I have some homework."

She gave a playful pout. "Okey-doke. Maybe next Saturday?"

I smiled. "For sure."

"Would you like anything? Plums, peaches, apricots, sunflower seeds? I can make trail mix."

"I'd love some oatmeal cookies and chocolate-covered raisins." I gave her a hopeful look. Why did I always feel a slight pang of guilt when I opted for cookies and candy over fruits and veggies?

She sighed. "Okay, but make them last. Last time

you ate the whole bag in fifteen minutes and had diar-
rhea for two days."

"Thanks for reminding me, Mom. "That's... yeah."

"No problem." She smiled and gave a wink before
twirling out the door.

Cool, now I had the whole afternoon to myself. I
blasted the radio and attacked my room. I organized
my cassettes alphabetically and used the white vinegar
and water solution my mom mixed in a squirt bottle to
clean my mirror. (She refused to use the "toxic" and
"overpriced" blue cleaner from the store.) I lined up
my nail polishes along my dresser—from light to dark,
hung up clothes, and threw out old stuffed animals,
saving only Raggedy Ann and the stuffed dragon I'd
won at Kennywood last summer.

Under my bed I found missing socks, markers,
pennies, safety pins, buttons, and a box full of beads.
There was also a balled up, dusty flannel I hadn't seen
for two winters, a fistful of Bazooka Joe comics, a pencil box full of Wheat pennies, buffalo nickels, a folded
up two dollar bill (Ooh!), a tin foil covered shoe box
that held old valentines, and my diary from sixth
grade. This cleaning was long, *long* overdue.

I sprawled across my bed and opened the diary to
a random page.

MALL HAIR MALADIES

February 14th, 1983

Dear Diary,

BAD DAY! Brian is totally lame! I thought for sure I'd get a card or something after weeks of flirting, but all I got was the same packet of Fun Dip he passed out to the whole class like I was no one special at all! If he had any kind of brain he'd know you don't give a girl a pack of sugar powder for Valentine's Day! Besides, everyone knows the only good part is the edible stick. And the last time I had that stuff I poured the whole packet of powder in my mouth at once and accidentally sneezed it into Denny Haver's face, which got me sent to Ms. Miller's office.

I'm just glad I didn't hand him the poem I wrote him, because today while we stood in line for gym, what did I see on his left hand? WARTS! Stacy said a frog had to have peed directly onto his hand and warts are totally catching—like chicken pox or poison ivy scab juice, so if I touched him I'll slowly turn into a reptile. Geez, you think you know someone!

Also, I think there should be some kind of complaint box or anonymous tip line to report teachers who torture kids for fun. I know for a fact Mr. Dish is giving way more homework than any other teacher in our grade. Maybe even the school, just because he can!

PS: I think I'm getting a sore throat. Told you this was a bad day. Thanks for listening diary.

Love,
Tanya Renee Sheffield

~ * ~

Feb. 27th, 1983

Dear Diary,

So, last night I had the most horrible nightmare and I think I know why. At skating, Gina B. told us about this dead ghost lady named Bloody Mary. She said if you stand in a dark room and say her name in the mirror three times, she'll appear. So, after we got to Paula's, Stacy wanted to try it. Well, I was against it from the start because the whole thing's plain ridiculous, but I said fine. So, Stacy, Paula, and I stood in her dark bathroom and said the stupid name three times. Nothing happened. We tried it again, then her dumb brother and his even dumber friend yanked the door open and sprayed us with silly string!

Stacy screamed bloody murder, and Paula chased him down the steps, causing him to run for the door, where he accidentally tripped and ripped through the screen. Those two started fighting, her mom was shouting swear words at both of them, and their two dogs were howling like werewolves.

Stacy was rocking back and forth, all wigged out, swearing, right hand up, she saw Bloody Mary appear. I didn't see any face in the mirror, but she had me all freaked out. After things calmed down, and we fell asleep, I dreamed this spooky lady wearing a wedding gown was standing over me with blood dripping from her head and an axe in her hand. I screamed and sat up, but no one was there. When I looked at the girls, they were sound asleep.

I had a hard time falling back to sleep after that, and in the morning, when I told them what I'd dreamt, they both swore they had the same exact dream! That's why I don't mess around with ghost stories and now I'll never get a good night's rest again, thanks to Gina!

~ * ~

KRISTY JO VOLCHKO

May 11th, 1983

It's impossible to do this much homework and have a life! Is my mom any help? No! All she said was, "It's really not much, Tanya. You should get into the habit of studying on your own anyway, it will take you much further in life. Then she goes, "Choose your battles; not every problem needs to be a war." Blah, Blah, blah. She should switch lives with me for a week and see how she likes it. Plus, I'm going to be a detective when I grow up. Or a spy. Or Wonder Woman. And I'm pretty sure I won't need to be an expert on tariffs, hieroglyphics, or ancient artifacts to catch criminals. Do you think I care which countries trade rice and beans for oil, or dig in the sand for mummies wrapped in toilet paper, wearing expensive gold jewelry? NO! Mummies are creepy.

PS: Please let me get an A+ on my math test Friday.

PSS: I think Mark Wells is a cutie-patootie (even though he has bologna breath).

I couldn't read any more. Was that really what I considered important? Mark Wells? What a dweeb! Last year he got suspended for leaving the school grounds at lunch because he had doggie-doo all over his shoe, and some kids started singing, shoe-be-doo-be-poo, where are you? whenever he'd walk by.

I finished my math and science homework and cleaned my whole room in under two hours. I'm a beast! (A beast without concert tickets.) I listened to the radio all afternoon and didn't hear a thing about tickets, only T-shirts and cassette packs. I called Randi, who was helping her dad at the store.

"Gattano's Nursery, how may I help you?"

"Hi, Mr. G. Is Randi around?"

"Sure is. All set for Earth Day?"

"Oh... I forgot."

"Well, stop on down for some sprouts and seedlings for your mom, on the house."

"Will do, Mr. G. thanks."

He's such a nice guy, always trying to share plants with everyone. He actually took the time to include small, green cards with bits of nature trivia with each purchase. One of these days I'd get around to introducing him to my mom. They both seemed to live on Planet Happy Hippy-ville.

Randi picked up the line. "Hey, chicky." It sounded like she was chewing glass.

"What time should I come over?" I asked.

"I'll be leaving here by 5:30. Can your mom drop you off around six? My dad's teaching some kind of fertilizer-compost class until eight, and I wanted to try calling for tickets as early as possible."

"Agreed," I said.

She started chewing glass again.

"What are you eating?"

"Carrots and ranch dip," she said. "Yom-nom-nom-nom-nom."

I laughed, knowing if I were there, she'd have opened her mouth real wide to show me all the chewed up, mangled bits.

"Gotta motor... customer. Bring your crimping iron and a quiz!"

"Kay. Bye."

I took out the Strawberry Shortcake bag I'd owned since the fourth grade, and crammed in jammies, undies, socks, an outfit for tomorrow, and the photo album I planned to reorganize later. I also threw in two magazines, a few tapes, and my craft box in case we wanted to make friendship pins or bracelets.

My crimping iron was already in my makeup case. It used to be one of Aunt Trish's travel totes before she gave it to me. It's totally chic, with black leather, gold latches, and had the letter T stenciled across the top on both sides. Good thing we share the same first initial. It's roomy, too. I can squeeze all my hair and makeup products inside and still have room for other accessories like my banana clips and jewelry. I loved this case so much I decided early on not to ruin it by covering it with stickers. You know, keep it classy.

Tonight was going to be awesome! I be-bopped around to the radio, rolled up my sleeping bag, and pictured the exact moment when we'd be caller ten. I wouldn't scream and go bananas like everyone else did. Sometimes, they sounded insane. I'd say thank you and be grateful and all but definitely play it cool. I just knew we were going to win those tickets tonight; I could feel it in my gut. And Monday the girls at school would be all, "We heard you and Randi on the radio Saturday night! Yinz sounded totally cool like college girls or something."

I absolutely loved sleeping over at Randi's. Her dad usually crashed early in his recliner with a newspaper, so we pretty much had the place to ourselves. We'd stay up as late as we wanted watching R-rated horror movies, *Gorgeous Ladies of Wrestling (GLOW)*, and stuff our faces with junk. They had the best stuff, too. Chips and dip, frozen pizza, fudge pops, licorice — you name it. It was junk food heaven. In the morning we liked to mix different kinds of cereals together, watch morning cartoons, then listen to and record our favorite songs of the week from the Top 40 countdown. No matter how old I got, there'd be nothing like a good bowl of cereal and some *Looney Tunes*.

I sat at my desk and wrote out a quiz. Homemade ones were way more personal than the magazines. After we answered the questions we had to write whatever boy's name we liked at the moment and do a numerology compatibility. I picked Ryan Dietz this week because we had to choose someone from our school. He wasn't gorgeous like Jay Garrick, but I sat directly behind him in Social Studies, and, Thursday, when he opened a pack of multi-colored erasers, I thought it was sweet that he turned around and offered me a pink one.

I said, "Sure, thanks."

When he handed it to me his thumb grazed mine, and he smiled, giving me wicked butterflies, and his ears turned scarlet. Thinking of it two days later still made my stomach flutter. I picked my teeth with the end of a paperclip and stared out the window into the bluest sky ever. Yes, he'd definitely won a spot in this week's quiz, and in my heart—a king of hearts.

Memory Lane

*D*idn't they say listen all weekend for tickets?" I asked, as I chomped a Bugle corn chip off each of my fingers. We'd been listening for two hours straight and nothing. "Maybe it's a trick just to get us to listen only to this station."

Randi, who was curled up in the corner of her bed answering quiz questions, adding numbers with her fingers, and letting out a laugh here and there, looked up and said, "The night's still young, Tanya-toon." She chuckled. "By the way, your quiz questions this week are totally mental."

"Yeah, they're meant to make you think *really* deep." I stopped to listen to some maniac going psycho over free movie passes to see *The Care Bears Movie*. I kid you not, the guy was losing his mind.

Randi said, "I'd totally see *Care Bears*."

I reached inside my pajama shirt, cupped my left armpit and squeezed down hard, making loud fart noises. "That's what I think."

Randi laughed. "You're seriously disturbed."

I had to agree. "I just might be."

I leaned over and grabbed a handful of marshmallows, wondering if we could survive a whole month on a deserted island with the stuff on the nightstand. Who knew? Maybe we'd do quite well with a boom box, mint lip balm, an emery board, a handful of cotton balls, a bottle of nail polish remover, a scented magic marker, two cans of grape pop, a box of cereal, a couple of Fruit Roll-Ups, a half-eaten bag of marshmallows, and a box of Bugles. Bugles were a *huge* favorite of mine. Not just for the taste, but for some odd reason I liked to stick one on the tip of each finger and growl like a monster before chomping them off. *Watch out for the finger-eating Bugle Monster, arggg!* I did it with olives and shortbread cookies too. Always have, and I don't know why except it's funny to me. Maybe I *was* disturbed.

I slid down to the floor and began laying out stacks of photos. I thought it best to categorize them from oldest to newest. Did I really need my class picture from second grade? Yep. Summer camp at age eleven? You betcha—memories were golden.

"Did you ask your dad if you could go to Summer Arts camp?" I asked. "It's for three whole weeks."

"Yep, can't wait."

I handed her the only photo I had of my father. "Guess who this is."

Randi studied the picture of him standing on a pair of train tracks, giving the peace sign. "You look like him."

I thought so too. He had crystal blue eyes (my own eyes), and his long, sandy blond hair looked like it needed a good washing. My mom rarely mentioned him and answered any questions I had with a neutral, lawyer-faced, indifference.

Randi set down her quiz. "Do you ever think about him?"

I shrugged. "Maybe a little on Father's Day. And I never got to participate in the father-daughter dance or field day races. It's hard to miss someone you've never met, though. His name is Ian Hoffman."

Randi studied the picture. "Does he know about you? What's Jackie say about him?"

"He knows I exist but not much else. They met at this huge concert in New York that lasted three whole days. Supposedly, they had the time of their lives and were crazy about each other. Afterward, she went to college, and he traveled around. They wrote love letters for a while, and he'd send her these little poetry books with pressed flowers between the pages."

Randi put her hand over her heart. "Oh, that's so romantic! What happened next?"

"Okay, this is the story I got from Mom and Aunt

Trish. So, after all this writing back and forth, spring break came, and she and Trish hitchhiked to this beach—Daytona, I think it was—to meet up with him and his buddies. They had a wicked good time and then headed back to college. Ian returned to his parents' house in Connecticut. Soon after, Mom started having that morning sickness stuff, and she wrote telling him she was... you know, preggers. He replied saying he wasn't ready to be a father yet, yadda, yadda, yadda, then stopped writing altogether. Not a word. So, that November, my mom mailed him my birth announcement, so he'd know my name and date of birth and all, and he sent her this letter with some quotes about past lives, future lives, cosmic lives—whatever—but dude didn't even ask how she was doing or if she needed anything."

Randi looked crushed. "Seriously?"

"Yep. And the rest of the letter's just as lame, believe me, total wacko. He talked about wild horses and having a wanderlust spirit and sent some song lyrics about some bird. Freebirds? Free a bird? I don't know. Anyway, all that really means is he wanted to wander around playing bongos and smoking pot. My mom once told me he was a sensitive, beautiful dreamer and everyone's path and journey is different."

"That's some deep, hippie stuff right there," Randi said. "I wonder where his free bird wings actually landed him."

I chuckled. "So, get this. A few years back, Aunt

MALL HAIR MALADIES

Trish runs into his friend at the airport, one of the ones they partied with in Daytona. He told her Ian was in Oregon, living off the land in some hippie commune. Ha! He probably has *five* wives, *ten* kids, and a billy goat for a best friend." I snorted. "My mother went to law school, and my father's a bona fide hobo!" I shook my head in disbelief. "Talk about opposites."

Randi laughed. "It could always be worse. He could be like Freddy Krueger or something."

"Well, that's certainly looking on the bright side—my dad's not a burnt up serial killer wearing an ugly sweater and razors for fingers." I rolled my eyes. "How'd I ever get so lucky?"

She giggled and handed back the photo. It suddenly occurred to me I'd never seen a photo of Randi's mother. Not on a wall, in a frame, or in her wallet. If she looked anything like Randi she had to be gorgeous.

"Do you have any pictures of your mom?

She nodded. "They're in a box in my dad's office cabinet." She rolled onto her back and threaded her fingers behind her head. "It's been two years since I've laid eyes on her—seems like longer though. When she *was* around she was either on the phone, rehearsing lines, or getting her hair and nails done at the salon, so I was always with my dad or *nonna* anyway. That's what I called my grandma: nonna."

"Oh, I like that. "Nonna," I repeated. I tried to say it like an Italian, but it came out sounding half southern, half British.

She was quiet for a moment then said, "She didn't even leave us a number to reach her, Tanya. And the last time I actually heard her voice was on the speaker phone in my dad's office. He didn't know I was home from school yet, and I heard her voice, so I got all excited thinking she was back from her trip. Soon as I got near his doorway I heard her say, 'I've decided to stay out here a bit longer and audition for the part of Lana in this new sitcom. It's unbelievable out here, Joe—a whole other world, really. There's plenty of sunshine, ocean air, sushi bars, and TV producers everywhere. My God, you can't even believe the—'

"So, he cuts her off and says, 'I'm glad the commercial's going well, Toni, I am, but will you just say hello to Randi? She'll be home any minute. She misses you so much.'

"So, I just stand there, waiting to see what she'll say next, and she goes, 'Joe, I don't know... I wouldn't know what to say. I'm no good at that kind of stuff. She probably hates me by now anyway. Just, give her my love, ok?'"

Randi shook her head. "I kid you not. I hurried to my room 'cuz I didn't want him to know what I'd just heard, and that's when it hit me—she wasn't coming back. And the sad part was, I wasn't even shocked or upset, as if her presence wasn't even all that... *present* to begin with."

She sat up and clasped her hands in her lap. Her voice quivered as she said, "She didn't have the guts to say goodbye to me. Just hopped a plane to California for some dumb commercial and never came back." She looked out her window. "I felt the sorriest for my dad because I was closer with Nonna and Aunt Rose anyway... but those two were high school sweethearts. He had to have been crushed."

"That's when he started putting all his time into growing trees and flowers. I think the whole gardening thing was healing for him, and probably the real reason we moved here to start a new life. Too many memories there, you know?"

I couldn't speak. I was afraid if I did, I'd spill out what I *really* thought about her horribly selfish, poor excuse for a mother. What kind of mother abandons her eleven-year-old daughter and husband in favor of chasing stardom? To be on a few TV commercials? I knew my mother would never do something so cruel. She didn't have a self-centered bone in her body.

Randi unwrapped a strawberry Roll-Up and carefully folded it into the shape of an airplane. (I didn't know you could do that!) I noticed Randi liked to eat when she was stressed or nervous, and it reminded me of her first day at Seaton when she chewed through three packs of gum in one afternoon. I was glad she was opening up about how things went down with her mother since she'd never brought it up. Ever.

She bit the wing off of her newly constructed, fruit plane and said, "It's like with your dad, he's simply doing his own thing. If acting in plays and modeling makes her happy then I'm happy for her. I do care about her and wish she were more interested in being with me than being an actress, but like my aunt says, she is who she is, don't dwell on situations you can't change, it'll make ya sick. I'm not even mad at her, just disappointed she's a stranger to me now and maybe always was."

I hugged Randi's foot. "Well, she's missing out on an amazing daughter, lemme tell you! And when it's time for you to pick out a prom dress or wedding gown, you can always call me or Jackie."

"Your mom is incredible, Tanya." She smiled. "And when the time comes for us to start driving, and you get a flat tire or something, you know you can call my dad. He'll be right there, tools in hand."

We linked pinkies. "Deal!"

Randi lowered her voice a few octaves, "I'm gonna be your dad right now. Young lady, finish that quiz."

I snatched the quiz off her desk and we both said, "Turn up the radio," at the same time. Then we yelled, "jinx!" Because everyone knows if you didn't say jinx when you and another person said the same thing, it was two years of bad luck, and you had to kiss the foulest, fugliest boy at school to undo the curse. Why chance it?

Randi went to put a frozen pizza in the oven while I wrapped myself in her fluffy down quilt and worked on the quiz Randi had made for me. I read over the questions: *not bad.*

MALL HAIR MALADIES

<u>Randi's Quiz</u>

1. Favorite colors? Coral/Salmon & Red

2. Favorite lip gloss and flavors? Licketty-Lipz / Cotton candy & berry flavors.

3. Last items you bought at National Record Mart? Tapes / Pat Benatar & Prince.

4. Do you know anyone who ate Pop Rocks and drank cola at the same time and lived to tell about it? Yes, Paula's brother, Matt.

5. Last boy you kissed. Who and when? Tell all! I haven't kissed a boy yet, just the back of my hand for practice.

6. How many piercings do you have? Two in each ear.

7. In your opinion, what are the grossest foods on the planet? Mushrooms, onions, all seafood, okra, dippy eggs, pig's feet, frog's legs, fruit cake, wax beans, liver, cheese from a can, and hotdogs.

8. Best foods on the planet? Pierogies, crinkle cut fries with ranch dressing, butterscotch pudding,

all cereal except puffed wheat, ravioli, rigatoni & meatballs, coconut cream pie, & oranges.

9. Last R-rated movie you watched and with whom? A Nightmare on Elm Street, w/Randi

10. Who would be your dream, celebrity prom date? C. Thomas Howell or River Phoenix.

11. What's your ultimate dream job? A Charlie's Angel detective or a spy.

12. In your opinion, what are the WORST horoscope signs? Sagittarius, and Pisces.

13. What are the coolest? Scorpio (naturally), Virgo, and Cancer.

14. Future bra size goal? Monstrous! Just kidding, any size boobs will be fine as long as I have some.

15. Hunkiest historical figure from our history books? Young Joseph Stalin or a young Franklin Roosevelt Jr. (Bangin' bods!)

Enter current class crush below. Assign each letter to a number, add numbers, & reduce to a single digit. If it's 25, add 2 and 5 to get 7, get it?

MALL HAIR MALADIES

A-1	J-10	S-19
B-2	K-11	T-20
C-3	L-12	U-21
D-4	M-13	V-22
E-5	N-14	W-23
F-6	O-15	X-24
G-7	P-16	Y-25
H-8	Q-17	Z-26
I-9	R-18	

1. He's your true love, marry him now!
2. If he's a two he smells like a fungus shoe.
3. Superstar kisser—wicked romantic!
4. He's got potential (eh).
5. Mama's boy—dump him!
6. Your future prom date and possible long-term beau.
7. Lucky seven, hunk from heaven.
8. If he's an eight, not that great.
9. Cold sore city, baby. Doomed for a breakup!

R-y-a-n D-i-e-t-z = (122)

(1+2+2 = 5)

I did the math and circled number 5. Mama's Boy! Well that figures. I ate a handful of mini marshmallows, washed them down with a swig of pop, and flipped to the back of *Teen Street* to check out my horoscope for the month of April.

> Scorpio: It's the year of the Ox, Scorpio, and you're happiest when you're making things happen, not just talking about them. With the sun in Aries, it's time to set the world on fire and make a move on that career change or secret love interest. Make sure that easily aroused temper and sharp tongue don't get you into boiling water. Ouch!

> Lucky numbers this month: 2-9-17-24
> Best color: Burgundy

Randi came back carrying a scrumptious smelling pepperoni pizza straight from the oven. It was pretty good except for a few frozen spots in the middle that didn't cook all the way through. That didn't stop us from tearing it up, though.

"Did you happen to read my horoscope for this month?" I asked, swallowing a mouthful of crust.

She plucked the pepperonis from her pizza and handed them to me. "Didn't get that far yet, why?"

I said, "First, here's yours: Virgo, trust your instincts this month as relationships and patience are put to the test. Take your time and think things through, for this isn't the time to make sudden moves. Home is usually your haven, but things shake up a bit during the first week, and you'll have to go with the flow or be swept downstream. Lucky numbers this month are 3, 11, 17, and 29. Says your best color is turquoise."

She made a face. "Peach is my favorite color; blue is for barf."

"Listen to this," I said, and read her mine. "What do you think?" I handed her the magazine.

She looked them over. "It *always* says for you to watch your temper like you're some kind of raging lunatic."

"I'm gonna do it," I said.

"What?"

"Just like my horoscope said... make a move." I gave her a mischievous grin and brought the phone over to the bed. "What do you think Jay sounds like on the phone? Where's your white pages?"

Randi squealed and ran out of the room. She was back in a flash, plopping the *Bell of Pennsylvania* down in front of me. "Are you seriously going to call him?"

I flipped through the pages. "Yep. You're the one who said I should start by saying hello. Well, *Bonjour! Hola! Ciao! Salaam!*"

She gasped. "Listen to what's playing! It's a sign!"

The intro to Blondie's, "Call Me" began the *exact* moment I opened the phone book. There was no ignoring such obvious synchronicity.

Randi nervously began untangling her mangled phone cord as I flipped through hundreds of stinky, inky pages that quickly turned my fingertips gray.

"Shouldn't you be talking me out of this before I embarrass myself?" I asked.

Randi cracked open a new pop and slurped the top of the can. "No way. Ask him if he's with Oliver."

I thumbed through the Gs and saw Garrick's Market and J. S. Garrick on Watson Drive. "Got it. Remember the house I pointed to with the white awning and a million rose bushes?"

"The one with the pool?"

"Uh-huh. That's his." I scribbled the number under my horoscope until I could write it in my journal tomorrow. "He doesn't even know who I am, and I'm calling his house? Is that weird? What should I say?"

"I don't know, I've never called a boy," she said. "Just act natural, like you do this all the time. Start with some purpose for the call. Just make something up, like, I may have dropped my wallet in the store and I was just wondering if you came across it. At least now you'll be on his radar and when you see him next you can say, hey, did you ever find my wallet? Of course he'll say no, but you can start a dialogue from there."

"Randi, you're a genius! He probably already has some gorgeous high school babe he's madly in love with, then here's me, this goony girl who sticks Bugles on her fingers and mini marshmallows in her ears, who's been gawking at him for the past two years."

MALL HAIR MALADIES

"Marshmallows in your—" Randi laughed. "Really? But what if he's been checking you out this whole time at the arcade, and you don't even know it, huh? You're only a few weeks shy of graduation and then you'll be at the same school as him. And lemme tell ya, he'd be lucky to speak with you, let alone date you!"

"Jackie says I'm not allowed to date until I'm at least sixteen."

"Talking to a boy on the phone isn't really dating. You can have friends that are boys, right?" She raised her eyebrows at me. "I think you're procrastinating."

She was right.

She grabbed my hand and stood me in front of her mirror. "Remember when we did February's *Glamour Gala* quiz about confidence? Neither of us scored through the roof, right? It said in order to start feeling fabulously fabulous, you have to look in the mirror at least once a day and say something you like about yourself out loud. Accept your quirks, flaws, and all. Now what do you see?"

"You mean besides the crater on my chin and a banana nose?"

She laughed. "Noooo! You're more than just your zit. Pick something you like about yourself—anything. You can do this," she nudged. "The article said to treat yourself like you would a good friend."

I stared at my reflection and saw teased, blonde hair and blue eyes that were traced with blue eyeliner and mascara, and light gold, shimmery eyeshadow.

Glitter sparkled across my chest, bracelets dangled from my arms, and hoop earrings from my ears. I looked like a Christmas ornament. I smiled, revealing straight, white teeth that never needed braces and dimples in both cheeks. Not *too* bad, I guess—except for the zit.

"I feel like a cheeseball, Randi."

"Say *one* positive thing about yourself, it just takes practice. I'll even turn around." She spun around. "Go!"

I knew she wasn't going to let up until I said *something*. "Uh... hello, me. I love your awesome hair and think you're a pretty decent person... kind to animals, old people, teachers, and the lunch ladies at school. You have the greatest best friend in the whole world, even though she's outer limits for making you gawk at yourself in the mirror like a wackadoodle-doo before calling a boy!"

She giggled and put her hands on her hips. "He'd be the luckiest boy at school to have you standing next to him. And I'd give anything to have your blonde tresses instead of this unruly lion's mane I'm cursed with!"

"Okay, I get it. Now hand me the stupid phone before I chicken out. And your hair is like a freakin' hair commercial. Stop."

I dialed the number and whispered, "It's ringing. I like your idea about the wallet thing."

A lady answered, "Garrick residence."

I cleared my throat. "Um, hello, ma'am, is Jay there?" I asked in a syrupy sweet voice I never knew I had.

"He's not in. Who's calling?"

Oh! Why hadn't I thought this through better?

"Hello?"

"Yes, it's... uh, Joan. Joan Jett."

Randi was laughing into her pillow.

I heard the woman give a snigger. "All right when he gets in, I'll let him know *Joan Jett* called."

I hung up and groaned. "Well that went well. At least he won't know it was me."

Randi laughed, "You are brave with a capital B, girrrl! Who answered?"

"I think his mom. She sounded too old to be his sister."

What a boring, blah night. No tickets, and I'd officially become a Joan Jett impersonating, prank caller. We cleaned up our mess and set up camp on the living room floor for our Saturday night movie. We were watching, *The House on Sorority Row*. I didn't know how long I was going to last though. I was already getting sleepy. I buried myself in my Snoopy sleeping bag with the eleven holes in it (I'd counted once) and mumbled, "Goodnight, Randi-roni." When I looked over, she'd already conked out.

Welcome to the Jungle

The second lunch bell rang as I shoved my books into my locker and plucked a couple of quarters from my change pouch. It was the last day of school before Easter break, and the halls reverberated with the rowdy hoots and yelps of kids excited for seven whole days off.

Randi and I usually grabbed a juice and cookie from the cafeteria then met up with the other eighth-grade girls in the third-floor bathroom. We wouldn't be caught dead eating in the cafeteria—the insane asylum.

Someone with *extremely* cold hands came up from behind and covered my eyes. "Guess who?" I already knew it was Randi, before she spoke, by her Giorgio perfume but I played along.

MALL HAIR MALADIES

"Um, Mr. T?"

Instantly in a goofy mood, I spun around and jabbed her armpit. That drove her over the edge every time, and she shrieked like a banshee, "Yeeee!" For some reason I get super silly when she's around.

I threw my purse over my shoulder, and we power walked to the cafeteria before the lines got too long.

Randi seemed extra happy today, I picked up on it immediately. "What's up?" I asked.

She smiled. "Well, for one thing, it's gonna be bombastic not having any school work for the next week."

I couldn't have agreed more.

"And guess what movie comes out this weekend at Star-Zan Cinemas, and *we're* going to see it?"

"Which one?" I asked, as we made our way through the crowd of lunatics.

"So, my dad's newspaper was on the table this morning, and I thought maybe I'd check out the listings for the week since it's the break and all..."

I raised my eyebrows. "You're killin' me here!"

"*Desperately Seeking Susan* starts Fridayyy!"

I screamed, "*Shut* up!" We'd seen the previews for it back in February when we went to see *The Breakfast Club* and went berserk. According to *Teen Styler* it had had pretty decent reviews so far.

"I'm *so* there!" I said. "Did you ask your dad about the concert?"

"Yeah, he said I can go as long as your mom's going. I'm not allowed to go without an adult."

I groaned, knowing my mom wouldn't step foot in that concert. And forget Aunt Trish, the fridge calendar said she'd be in Colorado. "Can't he take us?"

"Already asked. He scheduled spring gardening workshops that whole week and since people prepaid, he said he can't get around it."

Randi secured a place in line while I grabbed two apple juices and two oatmeal raisin cookies. I saw a group of the sixth-grade boys flinging pizza crust at each other like Frisbees and another kid dump pixie-stick powder inside a girl's purse before she jumped up and chased him around the table. I couldn't wait to get out of this baby school.

I set our snacks down on the counter and shook my head. "Did you see that?"

Randi nodded. "Mm-hmm."

I tapped my foot impatiently as Mrs. Helk (The Hulk) took her good ol' time replacing the cash register tape. Couldn't she have done that *before* the lunch period? We only had thirty minutes, and she was seriously cutting into my bathroom social time. I looked around at all the chaos. "Is it me or is every girl in this cafeteria dressed *exactly* like Madonna?"

Randi pointed to the table in the center of the room. "Check it out."

There wasn't a girl sitting there that wasn't wearing fingerless gloves, jelly bracelets up to the elbows of both arms, layers of crucifixes around their necks, and some even sported fake moles. The cafeteria was filled with a bunch of macaroni-munching mini-Madonnas. It was fascinating!

"It was *not* like this two weeks ago," I said. "This is mind-blowing."

Perry Weckler, who'd been eavesdropping, leaned over, "How can you see past all that skanky hair?" He slapped his leg and cackled obnoxiously. "I call 'em bimbettes!" He was always such a nasty person; it was hard to believe we were in the same grade. No one could stand him. I kept my back to him and ignored the fake barfing noises that grew louder and louder in his desperate attempt for attention.

I couldn't take anymore. I rolled my eyes. "Knock it off, moron. You're *so* third-grade crude. Grow up!"

He made one last barf noise then howled like a wolf. I bit my tongue because I didn't want to be mean and remind him that from first grade until sixth, kids had called him things like Tater Ears, Potato-Pancake, Mr. Tato Head, Glow-Worm, French Fry, Q-tip, and Mustard Man because he had so much wax buildup inside his ears they practically glowed orange. No one would even stand next to him in line. What right did he have to make fun of anyone when he had potatoes growing in his ears?

Our misery finally came to an end when we were able to pay for our goods and book to the girls' room. Our secret, packed-to-the-brim lunch haven was filled with its normal haze of smoke, perfume, hairspray, and hysterics. We were in such a hurry we burst in, forgetting to do the secret "I'm not a teacher" knock and heard the whoosh of commodes as paranoid smokers quickly flushed their cigarettes. They groaned when they saw us. Stacy put her hands on her hips, "You're supposed to do the knock, you scared the turds out of us!"

I blew her a kiss. "Sorry, I forgot."

She held out a light-blue and white pack of Belair 100's. "Wanna ciggy?"

I made a face. "Barf me out. I can't stand the smell of those things. Where'd you get those?"

She lit a new one, took a long drag, and attempted to blow smoke rings, which, instead, came out as shapeless tufts of stink. "My granny's fridge, she has cartons of them."

Randi took one, lit up like a pro, and puffed. She coughed her brains out for about a minute then gagged and spit in a toilet. I swear she turned green. "Never again," she choked out between spasms. "Gag me to death why don't ya."

We all cracked up.

Stacy said, "Did you hear about Cassie Harting?"

I shook my head. "No, what?"

"She got sent home this morning. Head lice."

I made a face. "Eew." I tried to remember if I had stood near here anytime recently. I didn't think so.

Over at the sinks, a few girls crowded around Paula as she attempted to pierce a third hole in her earlobe. She wasn't using a needle or anything, just pushing the earring right through the darn lobe!

Stacy rolled her eyes. "Just jab it though, it only hurts for a second." She pulled her hair aside. "I'm already on my fourth piercing," she bragged.

Paula took a deep breath as some girls began chanting, "Three! Three! Three! Three!" Her hands shook as she placed the gold stud over the ink-marked dot on her ear.

"Three, three, three, three!"

She began pushing, her eyes watering something fierce. She let out a high-pitched squeak, and I heard a gross, popping sound. "It's through," she breathed. "It's finally through." Everyone clapped. She walked around, giving each of us a look at it. I didn't mention that her left ear hole was noticeably higher.

Gina B. walked over with a girl I didn't recognize. A seventh grader? I liked Gina enough. She was a nice person and fun to be with but talking to her for more than a few minutes could get annoying. She used to talk normal like us, but then she saw the movie, *Valley Girl*, and all of a sudden, her pitch was irritatingly high, and every day it was, "like, duh, I'm sooo sure, gag me with a spoon!" I mean, we all said some of those things once in a while, but hers was extra thick and constant. I hoped she got out of that phase soon before I took her advice and gagged her with a spoon.

Gina said, "Tanya, this is Lisa. Lisa, Tanya. She's been at Seaton for, like, two months now?"

Lisa nodded. I waved.

"So, oh m' gawd, I was just telling her that you're the one who can, like, burp the alphabet."

I was at the mirror doing my lip liner and said through pursed lips, "Only to the letter P."

Paula, who was beside me dabbing alcohol on her new piercing said, "She does names and whole sentences, too. Tanya, give her a sample."

"Sorry, chickies, I only do it for contests and special performances now." The truth was, I hated carrying all the air around in my stomach the rest of the day.

"Like, please do it for Lisa," Gina begged. She's never heard you, and, like, if someone has that kind of a talent, I mean, duh."

Paula said, "Then just do her name... something small."

I made up an excuse. "I just ate a cookie. It's way better on an empty stomach."

"Wait, wait, wait," Randi said. "Why haven't I heard of this talent before? I'm your best friend."

I sighed. "Because If I don't push all the air out I'll be burping for hours after, like a freakin' windbag. It's no big whoop."

Paula told Randi, "Don't let her downplay it, Tanya's a legend. She's totally undefeated in the school burping contests—outranks all the boys, and even holds the record for longest burp ever recorded at Seaton Junior High. She has a special gift."

Once in second grade I burped Stacy's name to

make her laugh, and ever since then people have tried to break my record of getting to P and always failed. So far, no one's made it past E. Oh, they wanted to know my secret, trying everything from drinking different kinds of pop beforehand, combining Pop-Rocks and soda, swallowing air from a filled balloon—you name it. I'd never tell them just how easy it really was.

All you really had to do was open your throat and gulp as much air into your stomach as possible. When you were ready, you'd just slowly released the air, mouthing the word or phrase of choice. You had to pay careful attention not to cut the burp off before all the air was out, because if you did, you'd be stuck with it in your belly for hours and hours, and it was super uncomfortable. I had to admit, there *was* an art to it.

The chorus of pleases finally wore me down, and I didn't want to disappoint my fans, so I said, "All right, all right. Any requests? I'm only doing two."

Gina yelled, "Yee-hoo!"

The girls shouted silly words and phrases until I finally I decided on two sentences. The room got quiet as I prepared for my burps. Then I let it rip, "What choo talkin' bout, wasteoid?" Then I followed that up with, "Bloody Mary, Bloody Mary, Bloody Mary, Bloody Mary."

The girls whooped and cheered.

Gina jumped up and down. "I told you! Didn't I tell you? Is that talent or what?"

Paula smiled. "That's m' girl! She's still got it."

Randi looked dead serious when she asked, "And all this time you haven't been sharing this with me?"

Everyone giggled and went back to what they'd been doing. A few girls were at the far end of the bathroom were going over cheer routines. Tiffany 'Graffiti' Reagan went back to her stall art. Gina passed out Avon books with samples of perfume stapled to the back of an order form with her mom's phone number on it, and the rest of us worked on our hair and makeup. We had eight minutes left to curl, spray, tease, pick, crimp, tease, spray, pick. Our hair was our crown.

Well, everyone except Tiffany. She didn't care much about hair or anything else that didn't involve letting everyone know how much she loved Frankie Meratta. In her signature blue marker "I love Frankie" was scrawled on stall doors, picnic tables, track bleachers, gym lockers, and playground monkey bars. Her infamy had even made it to the morning announcements. Mrs. Miller's stern voice had echoed over the school PA system, "Graffiti and destruction of school property will *not* be tolerated, and I assure you that whoever's responsible will be disciplined to the fullest extent."

But the "Blue Marker Bandit" hadn't been caught yet. The funny thing was, since the announcement a bunch kids had started doing it as a copycat thing and were now using blue markers to write about *their* crushes. It was way out of hand.

MALL HAIR MALADIES

But Tiffany was beyond obsessed. No matter what stall you tinkled in, you had to read, I love Frankie, Frankie is HOT, and Mr. & Mrs. Frankie Meratta, as if we were all going to forget she loved this dude. Someone recently crossed one out and scribbled underneath, "Frankie eats hamster turds 4 breckfist." They spent a lot of time on it too, actually drawing a picture of what I assume was an attempt at a hamster with little droppings coming out of its bum. It looked more like a pickle with ears with a trail of pepper behind it. I thought it was hilarious, and that stall had become my new favorite to pee in.

The marker thing started after Tiffany saw Frankie and some girl from another school holding hands during a couples' skate at Spinning Wheels and she just never got over it. But what she was doing seemed a tad... unhealthy. And for the life of me I couldn't figure out what she was so gaga over. He was a Boogaloo for gawd's sake.

That's what we called all the wannabe break dancers who wore things like red, plastic jackets with zippers on them, high-top sneakers, and backwards hats. Some even wore a single, silver-glittered glove. After school they'd stand in a circle around a boom box doing the Robot or spinning on their butts over a piece of spray-painted cardboard. They took this *very* seriously. I'd watched them once or twice when Tiffany begged me to sneak over with her and watch him dance. He wasn't really good, but I thought it was brave of him to at least try. Practice makes perfect, right? Who knows, maybe he'd end up in one of those breakdancing movies one day.

Come to think of it, all the boys at Seaton hung with one group or another. Besides the Boogaloos, there were the Jocks, who traded sports cards on the front steps and played hoops or stickball at lunch and after school. They wore nothing but Pittsburgh sports gear and reminded me of a hive of black and gold bumble bees buzzing around school, spitting wads of gum and sunflower seed shells everywhere.

There was also a small group of Punks, who were a colorful blend of new wave, art, and rock. They drew comic books and other types of strange but rad art designs. They shaved the sides of their heads, wore two different shoes, and rocked tees that said Misfits or Ramones.

That crew sometimes hung with the Headbangers, who wore a lot of black, and were heavily into metal bands like, Metallica, Anthrax, Iron Maiden, and Black Sabbath. You could always tell by their T-shirts which band they'd seen in concert that week. They had awesome hair, too, and everyone knows how important hair is.

The group I pretty much *loathed* was the Preppies. Those flipped up collar, penny loafer wearing golf snobs *never* spoke to anyone they deemed unworthy and would actually sneer at you if you just said hello. It was like, pah-leez, get over yourself!

MALL HAIR MALADIES

My favorite bunch of all? The Nerds. I don't think I need to explain why they're called that by the Meanies, but I personally think they're the nicest, smartest, kids at school and, sadly, targets for the Preppies, Jocks, and Meanies. I didn't like it when I saw them getting messed with. They literally never bothered a soul.

Maybe that's why I liked Jay Garrick so much. Every time I saw him he was smiling and had a kind, mature energy about him I found attractive. He just seemed like a regular dude who worked stocking shelves, ate chili dogs, and played baseball. He didn't have a mohawk, wear glittered gloves, have his collar up looking down at everyone, and, as far as I knew, didn't doodle skulls in his spare time. The boys around here actually referred to girls as skanks and bimbettes. Seriously?

About two minutes before the bell, Randi was in a conversation with Stacy and Paula about meeting up at the movies Friday and skating on Saturday. Just as I was in the middle of applying another coat of mascara the bathroom door was flung open, and in walked Wanda and Terry Boyle. The Boil Twins, people called them, and they reminded me of that wrestler, Queen Kong. They were larger than ninety-five percent of the kids here since they'd been held back twice. Big boned and oily haired, they always wore head-to-toe black and misery on their acne-pocked faces. Besides having a reputation for beating up boys, smarting off to teachers, and always being suspended, they seemed to enjoy the fact that most of the school feared them. What were they even doing in there?

Then I found out.

One of the Kongs spoke. "Where's Tanya?"

Me? There had to be a mistake. I haven't gone near either of them since the fifth grade when I was forced into being Terry's field trip partner to the museum by a chaperone. She didn't utter a single word to me all day—not even a thank you when I gave her no-lunch-having-arse half of my peanut butter and jelly sandwich.

Randi and I looked at each other. Everyone else got quiet.

I waved my hand. "Yeah?"

She charged toward me aggressively, and I saw a micro look of surprise on her face that I'd stayed planted right where I was, not flinching, not stepping back even an inch. She got in my face. I didn't like that one bit and felt a surge of heat rise to my cheeks and my heartbeat quicken.

Her nostrils flared as she stared me down with her best, "you'd better be afraid of me or else" look. "You call my cousin a moron?" She barked. I could smell garlic on her breath. She reminded me of that raging bull on the *Bugs Bunny* cartoon.

In two seconds flat Randi was beside me with her arms folded across her chest wearing an expression I'd never seen. The other girls stood frozen like mannequins. It was intense.

I answered cockily, "Who's your cousin, and *is* he a moron?"

Wanda pointed her finger in my face. "Perry Weckler, you little bitch, and I'm gonna—"

Before I had a chance to react, Randi jumped in her face, actually putting her nose to Wanda's. Fire blazed from her eyes. "You'd better watch who you're calling bitch, *bitch*!"

Wanda flinched, and her sister moved a few steps closer to us. Five minutes ago, everything was normal. How was this even happening?

I dropped my purse to the floor, ready to deal with whatever might happen next. I knew from seeing them bully others, that the worst thing you could do was act afraid. They loved fear—could smell it a mile away. And I couldn't *stand* bullies! I raised my voice twice as loud as Wanda's and made sure I emphasized the word moron. "I called him a moron because he is a moron. So, before you come in here running your big, fat mouth, you'd better get your facts straight!"

Her sister hung back, waiting to see what would happen next, and Randi looked fierce, ready for anything. I don't think Wanda was prepared to be challenged and it threw her off. She was used to kids cowering when she huffed and puffed, but she saw we weren't those people. Wanda took a step back.

Brrrrriiinng! Saved by the bell. Wanda looked from me to Randi and gave us both the middle finger before storming out, Terry in tow. My hands were shaking from adrenaline, and I was breathing fast. I never had anyone want to pick a fight with me like that before and I hadn't even seen it coming!

The girls whooped and yelled things like, "That was totally bitchin'! Holy crap! Freak me out! Psychotic!" They filed out of the bathroom, dramatically replaying the scene they'd just witnessed, word for word, "She said this, then she said that..."

Stacy had her hand over her mouth, her eyes as round as saucers. "That was insanity!"

Paula laughed nervously, "What is that psycho's problem?"

I said, "Weckler was in the lunch line making barf noises, and I called him a moron."

Paula rolled her eyes. "That whole family is a bunch of whack jobs."

Randi, who was always so calm was furious, her eyes still lit up. "I don't know who she thinks she's talking to like that. Where I come from, those are fightin' words."

I added, "Those are fighting words *anywhere*, and you don't ever get in someone's face like that. They both think they're so tough, always pushing people around. Wanda just came off suspension for beating up a sixth grader! That's what makes *me* mad!"

The second bell rang; we'd be late for English. I was sure the entire school would catch wind of this, and then some, by the end of the day. Paula and Stacy hustled out the door with Paula yelling behind, "See you Friday night, you bad mamma-jammas!"

Randi and I just stood at the sinks calming ourselves down, neither of us saying a word. What was there to say? We simply gave each other a hug.

Dream a Little Dream of... Mean

*a*s soon as I got home I flung my purse over my desk chair and changed into baggy jogging pants and a sweatshirt. What a day. I clicked my clock radio on to the easy listening station and shut my eyes. I didn't want to think of anything—not the day, the tickets, or the weekend—just the sound of soft music playing. That was at 3:36 p.m.

The next thing I knew, I was aware I was dreaming. I was walking across a plush, green yard that felt like mine but didn't resemble my actual yard. In the distance there was a white gazebo and hundreds of flowers and rose bushes were everywhere. As I walked closer—without my feet touching the ground—I saw some of my school friends playing volleyball. Stacy was puffing on a cigarette and blowing heart shaped smoke rings, Mr. T was handing out rainbow-colored snow cones, and Aunt Trish was swinging from a tree like Tarzan.

Randi waved me over to the gazebo where someone beside her was barbecuing on a grill. I walked closer, hoping to score a cheeseburger or something and saw it was Randi's dad holding the spatula. He flipped a burger ridiculously high into the air, and it landed perfectly on a bun. He smiled at me with such a kind, loving smile it melted my heart. He handed me a plate and said, "The potato salad is made with Miracle Whip, not mayonnaise, there's a difference, you know." I looked over at Randi and saw she was smiling at me in that same way, full of love.

Suddenly, the sky darkened, like it was about to storm, and Queen Kong charged out from the bushes wearing giant scuba fins and rabbit ears. Everybody ran screaming except me. I wanted to, but it was like I was frozen or glued to the ground. *I can't move!* I tried to scream, but my voice was gone! She inched closer... closer... she was right in front of me! But when I got a better look, it's wasn't Queen Kong at all, it was... Grandma?

That's when I heard Lionel Richie singing softly in the background, and just as Grandma was about to stomp me with her scuba fin feet I screamed and bolted awake!

My hair was stuck to my face, and it felt like I'd been drinking sand. My room was pitch dark except for the glow from the radio, where a Lionel Richie song was playing. 8:46 p.m. I couldn't believe I'd slept so long. What a dream!

Disoriented, I fumbled around for the lamp chain, and the sudden light made me squint. A glass of apple juice and some melon slices sat on a paper plate on the nightstand. I took a few sips of juice and a bite of melon and felt myself becoming more alert as I tried to interpret that bizarre nightmare. What was with the mayonnaise potato salad comment? Was it because Wickler had potato ears and caused trouble at school today? And Grandma/Queen Kong had on scuba fins? I must've been really out of it.

I got up, splashed some cool water on my face, and went to find my mom. The house was quiet. I shuffled my feet loudly to make lots of noise, so I didn't spook her by suddenly appearing in the doorway while she was engrossed in one of her novels. We had a tendency to accidentally scare the crap out of each other, then crack up while the other screamed in terror. I found her curled up on the living room sofa, eyes closed, towel on her head, and a cup of chamomile tea on the table beside her.

"Hey, mum."

She smiled. "You were tuckered out, huh?" She lifted the afghan. "Get in. How was your day?"

I snuggled beside her. "Same ol', same ol'." I

wasn't about to mention that petty bathroom incident. I yawned loudly. "Thanks for the snack; I can't believe I crashed like that."

She smoothed back the hair from my forehead. "You must've needed it."

I sensed something was wrong. She seemed moody, quiet, like she had something on her mind. She only got this way when... oh, no.

"Is Grandma Vera coming for Easter?" I asked, not really wanting to know the answer.

She nodded.

Nooooo! I shivered as my dream flashed through my head. It was going to be a rough weekend. I had no clue why she put up with that woman, mother or not. Vera had something awful to say about *everyone* and *everything* and being around her made my stomach ache.

Vera, the joy evaporator, had a knack for wiping the smiles off every face around her as if she truly received pleasure from making others squirm as she ruthlessly criticized their flaws. Aunt Trish called it *Schadenfreude*. I think it's supposed to mean you enjoy other people's misery or something. And she was a master at pretending it was all out of concern.

I'd seen it my whole life and had decided that when I was old enough to choose, I'd *never* be around her if I could help it. But Mom was always respectful, even though Vera behaved like a mean, spoiled, toddler rather than a mature, loving mother and grandmother. Then there were the excuses: Grandma had a hard life, she's just set in her ways, you don't get to pick your parents, and you only have one mother. And while Mom had one excuse after another for the vicious behavior, Vera was just the opposite. My mother could do no right, never did, never would, and she made sure *everyone* knew it.

"Jacqueline, your hair's too long. You're too old for that style. I guess you're just begging for neck problems. Are you getting pudgy again? You were much thinner at Christmas. Men prefer smaller women."

At Christmas: "Jacqueline, you're too thin for those slacks," a look of disgust on her face. "They hang off of you. Aunt Marge had that unshapely figure, too. Are you wearing a brassiere? You always did like a lot of attention. You get your stubbornness from your father's side. That whole family is stubborn as mules!" I didn't think my mother was stubborn at all.

"The food's too hot, too cold, too salty. Is this real butter or that rubbish spread? What is tofu anyway? That's not even real food. Sounds foreign to me. Why are you into the strangest things? Did you hear about your cousin Darlene? Chased another husband off, she did. Betty's daughter took her on a cruise for her birthday, and what did I get? A Topaz broach you know I won't wear and flowers that died three days later. I think you purposely get me things I won't use. Your Aunt Marge was spiteful that way, too."

On and on she spewed verbal daggers toward anyone in her path. Everyone had it better, the grass was always greener. She insisted things *only* happened to her and that she'd been cursed with the evil eye since childhood by an old neighbor woman.

I groaned. "But why?"

"Honey, it's Easter. We can't expect her to spend it alone, can we?"

"She's alone because she's horrible. No one else can stand her!"

She pleaded with her eyes. "It's the right thing, Tanya."

"I guess." I picked a few fuzz balls off the blanket. "Can I go the movies on Friday night to see *Desperately Seeking Susan* and then sleep at Randi's? Randi's dad can drive us, she already asked, and he said yeah."

"It's not rated R, is it?"

"PG-13, you can check. And we wanted to go skating Saturday afternoon, too."

She sighed. "I'm picking Grandma up from the bus station Saturday at noon and I'm sure she'd really like to see you and—"

"She's coming *Saturday*? Sleeping *here*?" Ugh, that was just two days away! "Why can't she stay at Uncle Doug's?"

"Because, Tanya, she was there last Easter, and it's our turn to—"

"To what? Endure the torture?"

"You're not making this easier. She's getting on in years, and there won't be many holidays left with her."

"Good!" I said, regretting it immediately. "I'm sorry. It's just that she's *your* mother, not mine, and you have all this patience for her comments; I don't. She literally makes my blood boil. I seriously just had a nightmare about her before I even knew she was coming. She was Queen Kong and had on these scuba fins and—"

Mom burst out laughing. "Who's Queen Kong?"

"She's a wrestler. Anyway, it was like I could sense her coming or something." I took her hand. "I'm begging you, please can I sleep over at Randi's Saturday too, after skating? That way, I won't have to be around her that much. The two of you will have some alone time, and she'll still get to see me for Easter, just enough so she can't complain about it, and we all win. I solemnly promise I'll help with anything you need."

"I hear you, okay?" She raised her eyebrows. "You're becoming quite the negotiator, aren't you?"

I shook my finger. "You're the one who always says communication and compromise are best, right? I dotted the tip of her nose with my index finger, making her laugh. "You're the best mom ever." And I meant it. I think it surprised her how fiercely I hugged her to me, but it dawned on me just how special she truly was. Not all moms were loving and kind, there to listen to their daughter's concerns or fears, or leave them bedside snacks in case they woke up famished from a nap. Some were cruel with their words or abandoned their daughters, breaking their tender hearts into a gazillion pieces. Yes, Jackie was definitely what Aunt Trish would call, the crème de la crème of mothers, and I was lucky enough to call her mine.

~ * ~

On Thursday, Mom took the day off from work for our annual Easter break shopping trip. She'd save the previous week's Sunday paper with all the sales flyers, and that morning we'd cut coupons and make out a list of stores we wanted to hit. Our first stop was always brunch—someplace we'd never been, where she'd encourage me to choose at least one item I'd never tried before. Last year I picked escargot, which wasn't half bad for being deceased snails. There was definitely a dirt aftertaste despite all the butter sauce.

Then we'd head to Kaufmann's to try on Easter outfits for wherever we were going that year—Uncle Doug's, church, Aunt Trish's, a charity benefit—it changed every year. After that, we'd cruise the stores for sales on shorts, tees, undies, and shoes.

That week, Horne's was having a sixty percent off curtains & draperies blowout and Mom wanted to replace the dining room panels with "something a bit lighter." Sears was having a buy one get one, half off ladies outerwear sale, and the flyer for Lerner New York said they'd take an additional forty percent of all winter clearance items, such as jeans, turtlenecks, socks, belts, and leggings.

Lerner was my favorite, but I could only afford to shop there with Mom. She'd give me a budget before we started, and I could buy anything I wanted as long as I stayed under that amount. So, if I chose really expensive jeans I'd only be able to buy two or three pairs, and not much else, but if I used coupons and bought only bargain items I'd get triple the amount of clothes—three pairs of jeans, shorts, skirts, socks, a swimsuit—you get the idea. We didn't spend like this all the time, I mean, we weren't rich or anything. Only twice a year did we go big shopping—once in the fall, for winter and school clothes, and again in the spring, for summer wear.

It felt odd shopping for bathing suits when it was thirty-five degrees out and snowing. I was waiting for just the right time to bring up the concert and I knew instinctively it was *not* going to be the weekend her mother was in town. I told Mom not to bother buying me an Easter outfit since we'd be at home with Vera. Why waste the money? I'd rather have a couple extra bras instead.

For lunch, I enjoyed Japanese cuisine for the first time and tried something called sushi. It turned out to be raw fish with rice and seaweed rolled neatly and sliced, and it was delicious! I even learned how to use chopsticks—after about fifty tries—but I was determined to eat sushi right. I tried some of Mom's shrimp tempura (amazing) and a sip of her Junmai Daiginjo

Sake—that's Japanese rice wine—which made me cough.

We also window shopped, browsed a couple of art galleries, and sat on a bench in Market Square listening to a very entertaining reggae band called Shabba-Rabba Ding-Dong. We shared a jumbo pretzel (most went to the pigeons), and I was glad I'd brought along my camera to get some good shots of the day. Mom thought it was funny I used up most of the film on the sushi and the pigeons.

We made it home a little after nine from a tiring, yet wonderful day, and by 9:30 I was pooped! I went straight to my room to put some things away that didn't need to be washed and called Randi, who'd been at the store all day helping her dad prepare for their Easter sale. There was no answer, so I took a hot shower, climbed into my jammies, clicked on B-94, and placed the phone beside my bed. I dialed the radio station and got through right away.

"B-94," a man said.

"Um... hello, I was wondering when you'd be doing another ticket giveaway?"

He laughed. "Well, you'll just have to listen and find out! Thanks for calling and listening tooo the Beee!" *Click.*

I sighed. Well, that was annoying.

Mom and I were getting up early to do some spring cleaning then tomorrow night was the movies. Since we weren't due back to school until Wednesday,

Randi and I thought we'd take the bus down to National Record Mart if we hadn't already won tickets. I was able to pocket $8.00 of today's shopping dough and tomorrow was allowance day. I had my ticket money! This was going to be the best week *ever!* Well, except for Easter with Vera. I couldn't stop smiling as I snuggled up to Raggedy Ann and drifted off to sleep.

I wasn't quite sure if I was dreaming or not, but I could swear I heard DJ Adam's enthusiastic voice echo from the speaker, *"Hold tight guys and gals for more chances to win those tickets... win those tickets... win those tickets..."*

A girl could still dream, couldn't she?

Blue Loons

*R*andi and I knelt before the gumball machines, fishing our treasures from the slots as we waited for the habitually late Stacy and Paula to arrive. I inserted quarter after quarter trying desperately to snag this gaudy, white ring with a pink unicorn etched on the top, having no idea why I wanted this thing in the worst way, or where I'd even wear it. But it said it was made from real seashells, so I thought it was kinda cool.

I didn't win the ring, but I *did* get a fluorescent green blob of putty slime that smelled like chemicals. What do they think kids are going to do with a hunk of goo? I'd bet my mother could spout off every toxic ingredient in that thing, too. I threw it in the garbage and wiped my hands on my pant leg. I also scored a strip of fake clown tattoos, a tie-dyed, rubber bouncy ball, a pretend $100 bill, a plastic mustache, and a black spider ring. I wasted a whole $1.50 on this bogus, yet strangely entertaining junk.

Paula and Stacy burst through the doors dramatically, and, as soon as they spotted us, Stacy squealed, threw her head back, and spun around in circles. Everyone in the lobby turned to witness her maniacal entrance. "Freak me *owwwwt*, I cannot *wait* to see this *movieeee!*"

Paula bounced up and down from one leg to the other, drawing even more attention. "And the concert, ahhh!" I couldn't believe they were spazzing out like that in the middle of a theater lobby. There was a little kid nearby, half their age, just standing there, being all good, watching my thirteen-year-old friends act like lunatics. They couldn't care less who was watching or how loud they were, either.

Randi laughed. "How much sugar have you consumed this evening?"

Paula whipped out a huge bag of mixed candy, her eyes practically crossing. She reminded me of that Road Runner character with her quick and jumpy movements. "I've already eaten all the taffy melts. *Meem-Meep!* Open your purses, I'll fill you up. *Meem-Meep!*" She dumped enough candy in to last us a month. It looked like I'd gone trick or treating.

"Thanks." It really was better to bring your own treats; the snack bar was pure robbery.

Stacy cackled. "I saw your honey-bunny at the store, Tanya. He was doing a spectacular job stacking the hot dog buns." She made a circle with her thumb and index finger then pushed her other finger in and out, making a very obscene gesture.

"Uh! You're a total puke-oid, you know that?" I flicked her arm.

She smiled wickedly, "I know."

Thankfully they calmed down when we entered the theater; I didn't want to miss a moment. We marched all the way up to the back row, and it was no accident I sat on the aisle seat *far away* from Stacy, with Randi to my right, and those two on *her* right—plenty of room for each of us to have one empty seat between us. We took up eight total, which was fine because most people seemed to be seeing *Police Academy 2, Friday the 13th, A New Beginning, Ghoulies, Vision Quest,* or *Breakfast Club* anyway.

We munched our candy, completely mesmerized by the story, the music, and the wicked-cool characters. I took in some new ideas for outfits and thought I might try that French twist hairstyle Susan wore in the bar scene. The movie was so awesome that the girls totally behaved themselves and didn't annoy me once. We left the theater singing "Into the Groove" at the top of our lungs, not giving a hoot who heard.

"That was the best flick *ever!*" Stacy gushed, "Gawd, did you see those earrings?"

We stood shivering at the curb, waiting for our

rides. How was it still this cold in April? Spring break, my butt!

Paula said, "And that pyramid jacket, I *have* to have it. It's gotta be custom made though. Like, I've never seen it at Fashion Bug or anything."

I giggled. "I loved the part when Susan dried her armpit over the bathroom hand dryer. She does the best stuff!"

Randi was looking at me strangely and I thought it was because of what I'd said, but she said, "Tanya, look in the mirror. Your tongue... it's blue."

I whipped open my compact and stuck out my tongue. Blue was an understatement! The inside of my mouth looked like I'd eaten a box of navy crayons, and my teeth were dark green! Paula's crazy candy! "What the hell, Paula?"

We stood at the curb passing the compact around with our blue tongues hanging out like weirdoes. I hoped we didn't see anyone we knew.

Stacy dug through her purse. "Which candy was it?"

Paula said, "I only ate taffy and Fuzzy Fizzers and I'm blue too."

Randi dug a Fuzzy Fizzer out of her purse and tore it open. Sure enough, it was a bluish-purple color. I wasn't sure exactly how many I'd eaten because it was dark in the theater, and I'd been engrossed in the film. I'd bet it was the candy with the sour cough syrup tasting center.

Stacy said, "I hope it's not poison, like, ink or something."

Paula rolled her eyes. "Take a chill pill, it'll go away after we brush our teeth. I didn't even know they did that."

We stuck our tongues out and crossed our eyes, making monster noises. "Blarghh. Fraah. Yaww. Grrrr-raw-ha-ha."

Randi blew into her hands and rubbed them together, trying to keep warm. "What time are yinz gonna be at Spinning Wheels tomorrow?"

Stacy bit the head off a jumbo-sized gummy bear and said, "We're gettin' dropped off for the 3:30 to 7:30 skate. Gina B's little brother is having his birthday party there and she said we could all stop by for cake since we're personal friends of hers."

We nodded.

Mr. G. pulled up to the curb and we waved goodbye and hopped in the back. Randi yelled out the window, "See you tomorrow! Thanks for the ink!"

I couldn't wait to brush my teeth and get the yuck out of my mouth. Who purposely made candy like that?

Mr. G. slid a Billy Joel eight-track into the player and asked, "So, what's the consensus, girls? Was it Oscar worthy?"

Consensus? What was that? Randi and I fell into a giggle fit and once we started, we couldn't stop. We stuck out our blue tongues and told him the story, but he only nodded with a puzzled look on his face. I wore my spider ring and fake mustache while we played "which hand?" with the rubber ball and sang the chorus to all the songs we knew with the word blue in it. "Blue Monday," "Blue Moon," "Blue Bayou," "Blue Jean," and "Bellbottom Blues." I got the feeling he felt like an alien when we were around.

When we got to Randi's, her dad ordered us meatball hoagies and said he had some paperwork to do before tomorrow's sale, disappearing into his den with a newspaper and stinky salami slices on a wooden cutting board. I wondered if Randi realized just how much he resembled Tony Danza, the dad from that show, *Who's the Boss?* Randi even looked like his TV daughter, Alyssa Milano.

I called my mom to let her know we were back at Randi's and that the movie was as trippindicular as expected. She was playing records, hanging up her new curtains, and preparing food for the weekend. I figured she might be working off some anxious energy about Vera's arrival.

I got out my toothbrush and brushed harder and longer than I ever had before, but it made very little difference. I wondered if something like this could be permanent. I stuck my tongue out at Randi. "Looky."

She smiled blue. "It'll be gone by morning, you'll see."

We spread our blankets and pillows out on the living room floor with our hoagies and a choice of three cable movies. *Poltergeist, Escape from Alcatraz,* or *Cujo.* We had seen *Poltergeist* a bunch of times already, and I wasn't too interested in the prison film, so we decided on *Cujo.* I gave it an A+, especially the end, but I'd never look at dogs the same way again. I decided then and there that tomorrow I'd locate an encyclopedia and find out all I could about that rabies disease. My neighborhood was full of dogs, and you could never be too careful. What if Goober next door went bonkers and bit me? Yes, I'd definitely be looking further into this.

Saturday morning, we slept in way later than usual and lounged around watching cartoons, only getting up to use the bathroom or get more cereal. It felt good doing absolutely nothing. I didn't forget to check my tongue though, and it was still as blue as a shin bruise.

Around noon, a tiny bit of guilt crept in because at that moment, it was very likely my mom was being insulted in some fashion, and here I was having a relaxing day. But I quickly pushed the feeling aside knowing it wasn't *my* fault Vera was mean, and *I* hadn't invited her to Easter. We all make choices.

After watching *The Smurfs, Muppet Babies, Alvin and the Chipmunks, The Get Along Gang,* and *American Bandstand,* we decided to stop being lazy blob-slobs and get showered and dressed. As I was sitting on the toilet blow drying my hair (upside down for maximum volume), Randi came in and handed me a five dollar bill.

"Five smackeroos!" I said. "What's this for?"

She smiled. "My dad left a note."

She read:

Girls,

Left early for the store. There's a fiver for each of you on the table. Bus fare and today's skate is on me.

Enjoy your day!
Dad

"Your dad is mega-supreme."

"He totally is," she said. "I was feeling bad earlier 'cuz I'm lying around watching cartoons while he's training two new employees and answering orders and stuff."

I smiled. "I was feeling that too, with Vera being in town and Mom doing all that cooking an' all. But what can we do? They could be here watching cartoons too!"

Randi said, "Exactly."

It occurred to me that Randi's dad would be at the store most of the day tomorrow for the Easter Sunday Flower & Shrub Bonanza. The *Pittsburgh Press* did a full-page spread about it and everything. A photo of Mr. Gattano's smiling face holding up a mixed bouquet was at the top, with an article about the store and a 25% off coupon underneath. It was rad.

"Where will you be tomorrow?"

She spoke out the side of her blue mouth while applying blue mascara. "At the store, why?"

"It's Easter, that's why."

"I know, my aunts were making a big whoop about us not coming up, but it's such a long drive. We would've had to leave today and miss the sale, and I wanted to go skating and get our tickets Monday."

"Come over for dinner. Even if it's for an hour... you can meet Vera."

"Ah, the infamous Vera." She had a twinkle in her eye. "Okay, what time?"

"Yay! I don't know yet. Will it be all right with your dad?"

"Of course. He already feels terrible about me being at the store on Easter, even though I volunteered. He'll be stoked I'm having ham with you guys." She smiled. "I'm glad you asked."

"It'll be an eye-opening experience to say the least," I promised. "Vera's something you have to see with your own eyes to believe. My description doesn't do her justice. But a warning... just like that hurricane ride at Kennywood, enter at your own risk, keep all arms and legs inside, and hold on for dear life!"

Randi put up her thumbs. "Got it."

Later, as I stood outside Garrick's Market waiting for the "coast is clear" signal from Randi, I chewed down two of my longest, most prized fingernails. We needed change for the bus, and since I wasn't looking my best with the blue tongue and all, Randi went in to scope out the scene. I peeked in to see her waving to me from between the cupcakes and loaves of bread. I sauntered in nonchalantly, loving the feeling of Jay's presence all around. His sister, Robin, sat on a stool behind the counter, engrossed in the book *Forever* by Judy Blume. I'd heard about that book from some of the girls at school. Supposedly it had a few "mature" scenes, if you catch my drift (wink wink).

I grabbed a pack of gum and set it on the counter. "Can I have change for a five, please?"

"All quarters okay?"

"Sure, thanks. Do you have an extra bus schedule?"

She reached behind the counter and handed me the 44S-South Hills, which covered most Mt. Lebanon and Castle Shannon stops. "You can keep it," she said.

"Thanks. And congrats on the basketball thing, that's pretty stellar."

Her face brightened instantly. "Yeah, I'm pretty psyched." She rolled her eyes. "My dad's telling *everyone* that comes in here."

I guess she figured that's how it got back to me, this random customer-stranger. It didn't take long for gossip to spread like wildfire around here. But I'd probably tell everyone too if it were my kid.

"Will you be out of state?" Randi asked.

Robin handed me my change and rang up Randi's

apple lollipops. "No, I'll be at State College, like, two and a half hours away but I'll come home for semester breaks and holidays when I can. I leave in July for preseason guard training."

You could see in her face how excited she was, and I was happy for her. I loved when people were passionate about something. "That sounds awesome," I said. "If I don't see you before you leave, good luck and have a tubular season."

"Thanks. Happy Easter!" she called as we rolled out the door.

When we were out of earshot Randi said, "It's good to see you and your future sister-in-law getting along so nicely."

"Ha! If only..."

Twenty minutes later we stepped off the bus across the street from the skating rink. We were pleasantly surprised to find Paula and Stacy already inside renting skates. They'd even taken the time to secure us a table and lockers, which wasn't easy given the place was surprisingly packed for a holiday weekend.

As I sat on the wooden bench lacing up my wheels, I tried to remember the last time I'd actually hung out here on a regular basis. I knew for sure my entire sixth-grade year was devoted to this place, and all the kids from different schools in the South Hills area had congregated here for food, fun, video games, music, and socializing—that is, before the malls and arcades took over. That was also the year Stacy, Paula, and I chore-ographed a roller skate dance routine to the song "Boo-gie Oogie Oogie." We practiced every day after school on the basketball courts until we were satisfied we knew every move by heart. That Saturday, Paula put in the request to the DJ and we tore up the floor! For weeks after, a pack of fifth-grade girls brought their skates to school and chased us down until we finally gave in and taught it to them. It was an easy dance to learn, and they, in turn, taught it to their friends. Now anytime DJ Beezy played that song, about thirty of us rocked the rink to the brink! I wish Randi had lived around here then. She'd have had a blast.

Another thing I loved about Spinning Wheels was how the DJ played such a huge variety of 70s disco mu-sic as well as the current 80s stuff. There was some-thing so exhilarating about skate-dancing full speed to your favorite beats while the cool air fanned your sweaty face and mirrored globes gleamed from the ceiling, creating sparkles of light everywhere. For a few hours on Saturdays, it was like I'd skated into another world. A world without math quizzes, socks to put away, or peas to eat—just my wheels, the lights, and some bitchin' beats. I was going to have to start coming more often.

The four of us trekked upstairs to the party area to see if Gina wanted to come skate with us. She did, of course, want to break away from helping six-year-olds pin the tail on a donkey. We all held hands and skated to "The Loco-Motion," "The Hokey Pokey," and "The Hustle." We went berserk when "Let's Go Crazy," "Funkytown," "Double Dutch Bus," and "Mickey" came on. All the ladies skated in a giant circle doing the robot when the DJ played "Freak-A-Zoid."

After a while we headed back upstairs to sing "Happy Birthday" to Gina's brother Louie and stuff ourselves with cake and ice cream. By then the rest of her family had arrived; two more brothers, three older sisters, cousins, aunts and uncles, their spouses and kids. I thought Gina was lucky to have such a huge family, and when I told her that she said, "Like, trust me, I wish I were an only child! You have to share everything, there's never time for yourself, and getting into the bathroom's a total nightmare."

Sometimes, when I lay on the couch after school eating apple butter toast and watching *Brady Bunch* reruns (one of my favorite shows) I couldn't help feeling a little lonely and wished I had a brother or sister to play games with on Christmas morning or read a bedtime story to. I'd always wished I had a "Brady Bunch" kind of family, but you get what you get, I guess.

The hours flew by, and I'd laughed so much that day my stomach muscles ached, especially when Gina's gram and pap got into a cake battle like two kids. They were adorable, and just the way I hoped to be when I was antique. Fun!

Before I knew it, we were hopping in the back of Paula's mom's station wagon for a ride to Randi's. We said our goodbyes and thank yous, and told the girls we'd see them on Monday. They'd decided to join us downtown so when we bought tickets, our seats would all be together.

When I called my mom to say goodnight and ask her to set another plate for supper, she spoke in a low, tight voice that sounded as if she'd already been put through the ringer. "Honey, you know Randi is *always* welcome, it's just... do you think it's a great idea under the circumstances?"

"Yeah, Mom, I do. She's my best friend and her being at the store tomorrow, even though she says it's fine, doesn't seem right. You know, life doesn't stop because Vera's in town. I swear, everyone walks on eggshells around her."

I was glad Randi was in the shower and not around to hear this. I wouldn't want her to feel unwelcome. "I'm not trying to be difficult, Mom, but it's not *just* Vera's Easter, it's also mine, yours, and Randi's."

She sighed. "Okay. At least... warn her a little."

"Done. What time should we be outside?"

"I'll honk at 12:30 sharp. Oh, Aunt Trish might stop over, if she can make an early flight out of Baltimore."

"Cool. Thanks, Mom. I love you."

"Love you too. Goodnight."

I belly flopped across Randi's bed and opened up *Teen Bell* magazine to the article I'd marked about homemade cosmetics. When I heard the shower stop I called through the door, "Hey, you want me to put a tray of tater tots in the oven?"

"Yeah. Not the garlic ones though... disgusting."

"And can I grab an encyclopedia out of your dad's office?"

"Sure, he won't care."

I dumped the entire bag of tots onto a cookie sheet, turned it up to 425, and went down the hall to Mr. G.'s office. I knocked softly on the door that was always kept closed and crept in, feeling like an intruder even though I had permission to be there. The room had a kind of earthy smell, a mix of leather and something else... wood? It was cozy, with a brown, leather recliner and oak bookshelves filled with books on trees, plants, gardening guides, military history, and classic literature. Framed black and white photos of relatives from Italy hung on the wall behind his desk. I especially liked the frame with his parents' immigration certificates and a single dollar bill. Randi said there was a whole story behind that dollar, but she forgot. There were also two spider plants and a large fern hanging in the window.

I told him once, "You sure do like plants."

He patted his chest, inhaled deeply, and said, "Plenty of good oxygen."

I plucked Volume 16, Q-R of the *Encyclopedia Earth Book* from the shelf and sat in his chair. I flipped through the pages: rabbi, rabbit, rabble, ah—rabid, rabies. There was a whole page about it with pictures of bats and some poor little dog with its eyes all yucky and swollen.

RABIES- (ray-beez) n~

A viral disease... blah, blah, blah... acute lyssavirus... blah, blah... bats... brain inflammation... nervous system. Symptoms include: Fever, headache, confusion, violent spasms, fear of water (*seriously?*), paralysis, fever, anxiety, difficulty swallowing, agitation, insomnia, abnormal or paranoid behavior, coma, death...

"Whatcha looking up?" Randi walked in, brushing the tangles from her damp hair with a wide-tooth comb.

"Did you know that rabies can be transmitted by the bites of bats, monkeys, cats, foxes, skunks, cows, wolves, dogs—"

Randi laughed. "I knew that movie was gonna jack you up."

I set the book back on the shelf. "It would take *weeks* of painful *and* expensive shots to combat this before we even showed signs, and if you get bit and don't receive treatment, you turn into a total wacko-loon before you're dead meat."

"Dead meat, huh? Well, then I guess we'd better not chat with bats who sit on mats and rats who spat on cats that shat on hats with fat—"

"Stop, crazy!" I laughed. "I think our food's done."

We sat at the kitchenette gorging on gourmet tater

tots—once regular tots until we stepped it up a notch with separate paper plates of barbecue sauce, ketchup, ranch dressing, and honey mustard. Voila: gourmet tater tots.

I showed her the 'Do-It-Yourself Kool-Aid Lip Gloss' article. "What do you think? Looks easy enough, right?"

Randi said, "Oh, yeah! Get it? The Kool-Aid dude goes 'ohhh, yeah' before he bursts through the wall, knocking all your stuff to the floor."

I laughed. "Yeah, some poor, unsuspecting chick's just sitting at her dressing table brushing her hair, humming to herself, 'shoo be dooo, doo be da,' and *kablam*, a giant, glass pitcher of red sugar water comes crashing through the wall all excited to give her a drink. *Oh, yeah!*

"The girl screams. 'Are you freaking nuts, man? Some kind of sicky? Get outta my room, creep-a-zoid!' Then she picks up a hammer—one just happens to be lying right there—and threatens to smash his glass to smithereens. Kool-Aid dude runs for his life as red water is sloshing all over the floors and walls.

"And the chick keeps screaming, 'You come back here! You're patching that hole before my parents get home!' He's running all the way down the road and she's *still* yelling. 'And who's scrubbing the red stain from my carpet, huh? Ya jerk!'"

Randi was laughing so hard, with her mouth wide open, full of potatoes, and ketchup dripping down her chin, I thought she'd choke. She gasped. "I can't... oh, gawd, I can't!"

"Don't choke on your tater tots (it came out *titty tots*), and you look like a rabid dog that just chewed off someone's fingers." That threw her over the edge and onto the floor.

I heard the garage door open and close, and then Randi's dad walked in and hung his coat on the hat rack. He smiled. "Hi, girls. Looks like you're having quite a Saturday evening."

We held our stomachs, in hysterics well beyond our control, and yelled, "Ohhh, yeah!"

The poor guy. No matter how hard he tried, he'd never get the joke when it came to us loons.

Our Lips Are... Peeled?

Before her dad headed off to bed I made sure to thank him for the five bucks. He was delighted, and a bit relieved, Randi would be having Easter dinner at my house. I got the sense that he wasn't a sit home all day, ham-baking kind of guy.

"Are all the ingredients here?" I asked, tearing the recipe from the magazine.

Randi took out a small pot and turned the kitchen radio on to B-94. We were still hoping for a ticket winning miracle. "If not, we'll improvise." She found an old canister of cherry Kool-Aid in the pantry and shook it. "Not much in here."

I said, "We'll make do. The recipe calls for two tablespoons of beeswax, two of coconut oil, two of petroleum jelly, and granulated sugar. It doesn't say how much, though. Simmer in saucepan, do *not* boil. Kool-Aid amount dependent on color preference. Meaning, if we want pink, we just use a little, dark red, more. We could add some of that glitter I saw in your drawer, too."

"Totally," Randi said. "We don't have to stick with the recipe *exactly*, it's just a general idea. We'll make our own formula... maybe even have our own makeup line one day and sell it to all of our fashion clients."

I liked the sound of that! "We'll be professional lip gloss mixologists!" I took a container of chocolate icing from the fridge and spooned some into my mouth. "We'll invent all kinds of cool flavors like, Bogus Banana, Cantaloupe Cootie, Cherry Chucker, Strawberry Slime, and Putrefying Pear!"

She scooped some icing with her finger. "Oh, those are keepers."

We stopped for a minute to harmonize to Bow Wow Wow's "I Want Candy." I sang soprano, Randi alto, just like they taught in chorus class. I put one finger in my ear like they do in the music videos or singing a cappella. Man, we sounded *amazing!*

I wondered what Jay would think if he saw me with chocolate icing on my chin and in my teeth, using a wooden spoon as a microphone, wearing a faded nightgown with holes in the sleeves. Then I thought, *who cares?* If he couldn't have a little fun and be silly he'd bore me to tears anyway. And everyone knows that future fashionista-mixologists don't do boring!

Randi said, "I'm not seeing coconut oil here." She went to the fridge and peeled the lid off a tub of margarine. "Think we could use this?"

"I don't see why not," I said. "And what's beeswax?"

She shrugged. "Probably just a fancy word for honey. I mean, what do bees make? Honey, right? Bees... wax."

"Oh, so when someone says mind your beeswax, they really mean honey?"

"Yep." She found a container of honey that looked well past its prime and squirted some in the pot. "What I don't get is, if honey's made from bees, why's it in a teddy bear shaped container and not a bumblebee?"

I said, "Because bears eat a lot of it." I poured in some sugar and a hefty scoop of margarine, not bothering to measure anything. Who needed measurements when we had common sense?

She said, "Next item on the list, petroleum jelly." She fetched a first aid box from the hall closet and counted out five packets of skin protectant and five of burn cream and set them on the counter. They were graying on the edges, sticky, and leaking.

I struggled to make out the faded words on the back of the skin protectant. "Water, white petroleum... perfect." I squirted them into the pot then read the back of the Quik-Care Cream, "Benzyl alcohol, water, aloe vera, methylcellulose, beeswax... hey, beeswax!" I added those to the mix as well. The Kool-Aid was so outdated, I had to chisel it with a butter knife and dump the lumps into the lip stew.

Randi, stirring with a wooden spoon, made a face at the yellowish-pink goop. "It doesn't look anywhere near red, and we're out of Kool-Aid." She opened the spice cabinet above the stove and pulled out all the red, orange, brown, and pink colored spices. "We'll just darken it up a little."

I sang, "That's the life of a mixologist. Our job is to find the perfect blend through trial and error, like they do at the lip gloss lab, right?" I peered in the cabinet. "Rosemary, oregano, cumin, thyme, basil... your dad's seriously the spice king."

"I know, right? On special occasions he cooks Indian food. He says it's good for the immune system and the soul. I think it reeks the house up like that one dude who's always on the bus... what's his face?"

"B.O. Billy." I wrinkled up my nose like I could smell him right now. Some smells you just never forget.

"Yeah, him."

Randi sprinkled chili powder, cinnamon, and a packet of hot cocoa mix into the pot. "If this doesn't darken it..."

Now, it resembled muddy sludge. "We need more red," I said, adding beet powder and paprika. It was getting redder, but *really* dark. It reminded me of the volcano pictures from my science book.

MALL HAIR MALADIES

Randi thought for a moment. "I'll bet something yellow will take the edge off that maroon."

I handed her turmeric, ginger, and curry because they were the yellowest, and she sprinkled some of each into the bubbling brew that smelled *very* strongly like... nachos? Tacos? Chili dogs maybe. The color was a now a nice reddish-orange. I hoped we could remember this recipe for next time.

Randi moved the pot to a cool burner and turned off the heat. "Time for the glitter."

"Not too much," I warned, "we don't want to overdo it."

"Us? Overdo something? That's preposterous."

I giggled. "How much do you think we should charge for our gloss? Homemade stuff *has* to be worth more than store brands, dontcha think?"

"I agree. Um... how about two bucks? And we have to call it something catchy, like a combo of our names. Ranya or Tandi."

"You *are* brilliant, Randi, you know that?"

We both got quiet, lost in our own thoughts as we cleaned up the kitchen and waited for the gloss to cool. The recipe said minimum thirty minutes to set.

Ranya Cosmetics. Tandi Lip Glossers. I could see every girl in school lined up outside the girls' room trying to score a tube. They'd say things like, "I'll take ten, please. What's your secret? Hey, I was in line first! Wait your turn!"

I'd hold up my hands and say, "All right, ladies,

there's plenty for everyone."

Randi would explain to them, as she signed copies of our bestselling beauty book, *Bodacious Beauty Tricks; Magic Lips & Fingertips*, "We simply can't reveal our secret ingredients, but I *will* say this, our magic gloss *is* intuitive. Whoever your current crush is, well... they'll want to kiss you passionately within minutes of application, guaranteed, or your money back."

Never once does anyone want their money back.

We'd be featured on the cover of *Teen Street* magazine, arms folded, sitting back to back atop the Empire State Building. Our hair would stay perfectly in place, not moving an inch, even though it's wicked windy up there. We'd explain our method in the chapter titled, "The Secret to Stiff Hair on a Budget." People will comment on how we could pass for fifteen or sixteen with just the right makeup, and the headlines will read, "Mixology Moguls, Randi Gattano and Tanya Sheffield, creators of RANYA, take the makeup world by storm!" We'll be more than happy to send free samples to Lady Di, Farrah Fawcett, Boy George, and each of the Charlie's Angels, as well as the top fashion models and department stores.

I was smiling from ear to ear as I dried and put away the last of the dishes. Randi went container hunting and came back with some tin ones that had once held sore throat lozenges. I figured once we made our first hundred sales we'd have enough dough to create designer tubes with our logo.

We filled the containers and placed them on a cookie sheet inside the fridge. Now all we had to do was wait. We headed back to Randi's room, and, right away, she grabbed a basket of jelly bracelets, knelt on the floor, and began separating them into piles by color. The girl actually cleaned for fun!

I admired how she kept her peach-themed room spotless with everything in its place—unlike my pig pen that I couldn't keep tidy for more than a week. Even the insides of her drawers, where no one could see, things were folded neatly, and color coordinated with little lavender soaps tucked in the corners. She swore it gave her clothes a nice scent, but I think she'd just spent way too much time with her grandparents.

She said, "I'm linking all my bracelets together into one long chain and hanging it along the ceiling. I dreamed the idea last night." She smiled. "Wanna help?"

"Nah," I said, sitting down at her dressing table and switching on the magnifying mirror with the lights across the bottom. "I'll help you hang it though, how 'bout that?"

I took out a Stridex pad and began scrubbing my nose. "You know, that commercial's so bogus. The girl wipes her face, and, like, there's not a single mark on the pad? You can *clearly* see she's wearing makeup." I looked at the one I'd just used on my nose and chin with disgust. *Yuck.*

"I agree, there's gotta be some kind of trickery going on there. And she never has any blackheads either. It's like, get real."

In our beauty book, I'd devote an entire chapter to skin care, with actual pictures of how to pop blackheads safely without scarring your skin. No phony baloney stuff just to sell books.

I studied the mirror closely, inspecting my pores, the insides of my nostrils, and my eyebrows. I smiled, checking out my teeth, then scowled at my blue tongue, which had only slightly faded since last night. I needed a change. Another ear piercing? A shorter hairstyle? Thinner brows? I remembered a photo I'd seen of my mom around my age wearing extremely thin, Twiggy-style brows. Mine were the opposite, too thick. I decided then and there I wanted perfectly arched, medium brows just like the models in *Teen Bella*. "Do you think my eyebrows are too bushy?"

"Your eyebrows are normal," Randi said, wrapping the bracelet chain around her bedpost, using it as a makeshift spindle.

I used a brow brush to smooth and shape them. "Do you have tweezers?"

"Bottom drawer, with the emery boards, I think."

I opened *Teen Bella* to the *Bold Brows* article and propped the magazine up against the larger dressing table mirror for reference. It said to use a pencil to measure a half an inch from the outer edge of your eye crease to your nose tip for the best angle. That sounded complicated, I hated math. I decided to skip that part and get right to tweezing. After a few failed attempts, I successfully latched onto a hair and tugged. That wasn't too bad, so I did another. That one stung more, making my eyes water. "Sss-ow!" I rubbed my brow. The third one made me sneeze, and my nose was running.

"This bites. There's gotta be a better way." I skimmed further down the page to "Wax Your Way to Wondrous Brows." "Randi, listen to this: 'You can have bold, do-it-yourself brows in as little as ten minutes with this simple sugar wax recipe. Simply heat two teaspoons of brown sugar and one teaspoon of honey in microwaveable bowl. Melt to syrup-like consistency, then allow wax to cool and thicken. Use a popsicle stick or Q-tip to apply where hair removal is desired. Place a cotton cloth strip over the area, applying even pressure, and smooth with your finger. Pull swiftly, opposite of hair follicle growth. Repeat as necessary.' Boom!"

Randi, engrossed in her bracelet linking, bedroom beautification project looked at me like I had three heads. "You're *not* serious?"

I smiled. "As a fart-attack. If plucking hurts so much, why torture yourself? Just skim and shape in one swoop, then rip it off like a Band-Aid. Trust me, you'll be begging me to do yours."

"Not likely. How 'bout we do more research first. What if it gets in your eye or—"

I held up my hand. "Relax, they sell this stuff at

Revco, except this way's more natural—chemical free. Besides, tweezing and waxing are practically sisters. It says here that this *widely* known method is used in the best spas across Europe. I'm gonna go make this stuff." I jumped up. "This is *so* going in the book," I said, as I ran out of the room.

I heard Randi yell, "What book?"

It was indeed *that* easy to prepare, and I was back in less than ten minutes with a steaming bowl of sugar wax and a popsicle stick. I had to chow down a fudge-pop to get the stick—all for the sake of beauty, of course. "I think the gloss will be ready soon," I said.

Randi was standing on her desk chair hanging the chain across the ceiling. "Cool, I can't wait to try it," she mumbled, her mouth full of thumbtacks.

She was *really* on the edge of that chair, balancing on her tippy toes, scaring the crap outta me. I stood beside her in case she began to teeter or needed to lean. "Please don't fall and crack your skull open. I already told Jackie you'd be coming for Easter."

She tacked up the last link, stepped down, and plugged in the clear lights she'd intertwined through the links. "There. What do you think?"

It was magnificent! The chain hung along the perimeter of the ceiling and met at the center. Each light reflected off a different colored bracelet, making the entire room glow like a rainbow.

"Randi, this is beautiful! I love it!"

She smiled. "Thanks. We can do it to your room if

you want."

"For sure!" I spun around in circles. "Now all you need is a disco ball for the middle."

"I was totally thinking that. When we go downtown on Monday, we can stop at that shop everyone's always talking about, Giggles Coop. They're supposed to have all that cool lighting stuff."

"I'm not allowed in there," I told her. My mom and I made the mistake of stopping in once and she steered me right back out the door. In the two seconds I *was* inside, I saw the raddest disco lights, posters, and lava lamps around. There were also glass cases full of freaky looking smoking pipes shaped like skulls, rows of switchblade knives, cigarette lighters, and packs of tobacco rolling papers. Wall-sized posters hanging behind the counter had big, green leaves on them and magazines with half-naked girls were stacked against the wall. The whole place reeked of some kind of strange, smoky incense I'd never smelled before, and clung to my clothing long after we'd gone. I thought we'd see lamps and purses, but this was... wow. My mom was like, nope!

She said, "Promise me you'll never go in there, Tanya. That store is... it'll get busted one day for... all kinds of paraphernalia, and whoever is in there when it happens could get in trouble *just* for being in there. Promise?"

I promised.

I rooted through Randi's desk for scissors. "Do you

have something cotton I can cut into strips?"

She opened a dresser drawer and handed me a white hanky folded into a perfect triangle. "Will this work?"

"Yep." I cut a few thin strips and stirred the wax with the stick. It was warm, but not too hot. All set to go.

My nervousness kicked into gear. "Will you put a tape on or something, please? All these radio commercials are annoying. And there wasn't a single ticket giveaway all night."

"What are you in the mood for?"

"Surprise me," I said.

Randi chose a mix tape. I *loved* her wildly unpredictable creations! Example: The tape would start with an Elvis song, then Prince, The Temptations, Led Zeppelin, Olivia Newton-John, Talking Heads, Pat Benatar, and Weird Al Yankovic. It was like musical Skittles.

"I'm doing a patch test on my arm first," I said.

She scooted her chair next to mine and studied her face in the magnifying mirror. "Good idea."

I smeared a small amount of goop on my left arm where I had the most blonde fuzz and placed the cloth strip over it. My years of practice with those Lick & Stick tattoos was coming in handy. If you didn't press down evenly or long enough, only half the tattoo turned out and you'd be stuck wearing what was supposed to be a unicorn but ended up as a headless horse.

I yanked off the strip, and it actually worked! I held out my arm. "Looky! It didn't even hurt."

I could tell she was impressed. "That's wild how it seriously ripped the hair right out of the pore." She touched the smooth area and inspected the strip that now possessed my arm fuzz in a glob of wax.

I'd use this firsthand experience for our chapter on hair removal—adding wax recipes, tips, and even throwing in the patch test suggestion. I was so excited. "Time for my brows!"

I spread a small amount between my eyes where there was a little peach fuzz, pressed the strip down and yanked. Smooth again. "Looks good, huh? I'm not shaving my legs for a whole week, so I can wax 'em next weekend."

Randi pulled up her pajama pant leg and inspected the stubble on her knee. "I'll give that a try. I swear, no matter how well I shave I can never get all the stubble off my knees."

I began with my left brow, more confident now. "I could do yours when I'm done, I'd be happy to—"

"What's wrong with my eyebrows?" She was now plucking random hairs from her knee with the tweezers.

"Nothing, I'm saying *if* you want," I said, spreading a thin amount across the bottom portion of my brow. I pressed, rubbed, and yanked, revealing a much thinner, slightly arched brow. "I can't believe I didn't do this sooner."

I repeated the process on the right side, spreading a thin layer across the bottom. but I was so focused in the mirror, perfecting the arch, that I mistakenly grabbed a used cloth strip with wax already on it and pressed down firmly. So, when I yanked, most of my brow came off with it!

Randi gasped.

I screamed, "What the mother f—"

"Tanya!"

I stared in shock at the spot where my eyebrow *used* to be and threw the waxy strip violently into the air. I jumped up and paced the room, instantly hysterical. "I hacked off my eyebrow! Randi, I'm gonna flip out!"

"It's okay, Tanya. It's all right." She flipped on the overhead light. "Oh my gawd."

I put my head in my shaking hands not knowing whether to scream, cry, or laugh at the ridiculousness of the situation. And I had no one to blame but myself! How could I be so careless? "I can't put *this* in the book," I mumbled in my hands.

"What book?" Randi asked again.

I flung myself on the bed like a two-year-old and wailed, "I *refuse* to walk around with one eyebrow, Randi. I can't go to school like this! I look like something from *Star Trek*!"

"You won't have to, Tanya; it's not all the way gone. It won't be easy, but we *can* fix this until it grows back." She sprang into action, opening drawers, plugging in the curling iron, gathering brow pencils in different shades of brown. "Come 'ere, lemme help you."

I wanted her help, I did, but I couldn't go near that mirror; I was hideous! She came over to the bed, where I sat, dazed, and began working her magic.

She spoke in a soothing voice while she worked. First, with different shades of eyeshadow, then the brow pencils. "Oh, yeah, that's... yep... looking good." She concentrated like she was doing brain surgery as she smoothed and blended like a pro. "Wait until you see this, you're gonna love it. You can hardly tell... really, like nothing happened. I'm gonna have to thin out the other brow, *with the tweezers*. There's no getting around it."

I groaned.

"I know, but we have to make them at least somewhat proportionate. And we'll fix your bangs to where it hides the bald... er, thinnest area."

I sat staring off into space, wondering how I was going to spend the rest of my life like Mrs. Spock. A side-show circus freak. Everyone at school will hear the story about the case of the missing eyebrow, and the meaner boys will call me things like Uno-Brow and Bald Betty. I thought about Mrs. Helk, the lunch lady who had no eyebrows at all, just two pencil slashes. Did she accidentally wax them off and they never grew back? I'd be like Helk the Hulk, only able to scoop creamed corn in a cafeteria because no one would hire a girl with one eyebrow!

Randi saw the terror in my face. "Tanya, look at me... it's gonna be okay." She hugged me, and I let out a sound that was a cross between a groan and a squeak. A greak.

She continued talking, busying herself with designing me a fraudulent, girl-made eyebrow and restoring my sanity. She said, "No one will even notice we drew on a faux. Eyebrows grow back super-fast."

"How do you know?" I asked.

"Well, you know how when you shave your legs, and it's all smooth, but if you forget the next day or have the flu or something it's like cactus limbs?"

"Yeah?"

"By the time Easter break is over it'll be growing back in, I'm sure."

She was making sense. My hair *did* grow annoyingly fast. I brightened.

She noticed. "Yep, three, four days *max*, you'll see. And I solemnly promise that we won't go to the mall, the park, shopping—anywhere, until you're presentable. Deal?"

"You swear you'll never mention this to anyone, even accidentally?

She pretended to zip her lips. "Not a word, my lips are sealed."

"What about our tickets, and Stacy and Paula? If they see my bogus brow they'll blab to everyone. I know it!"

She said, "So we'll go downtown *next* weekend

and just tell the girls something came up. It's no big whoop."

I smiled up at her. "You're a good friend, Randi. Seriously, the best. Thank you."

She patted the top of my head like she would a puppy. "Don't thank me yet, I still have to tweeze your other brow, so brace yourself."

With every hair she plucked, I winced and yowled. She had the patience of a saint.

"Wanna see?" she asked.

I shook my head, "Not till we're totally finished."

She started on my bangs, which, thank God, reached just below my brow line. It'd cover the area fine as long as I didn't move, talk, or breathe. She didn't give up though. She teased, feathered, curled, and straightened—anything to conceal the spot.

Suddenly, the arch of my foot itched like crazy. I closed my eyes and willed it to go away. Sometimes itches just leave if you think of something else, but this was getting worse. *Go away, itch, you're not real.*

"I have an itch," I whined. It was unbearable.

The curling iron steamed. "I'm almost done."

I tried to use my left foot to scratch the right, but she was standing in the way.

She said, "Okay, hold on, I'm taking it out."

The exact moment she began unwinding my hair, my reflex jerked me forward to scratch. *Tzzz!* The barrel sizzled my forehead like a hot poker.

I screamed, "Yoww!"

"I'm so sorry! Tanya, oh, jeez." She ran out of the room and came back with a can of frozen orange juice. "The ice maker's empty. Try this."

I touched it to my head. "Eeh!"

She opened her sock drawer, fished out a lime green sock with kitties on it, and stuffed the can inside. "You just need a buffer, that's all."

I moaned, scratching my foot as much as I wanted to as she held the kitty sock orange juice can to my head. "Thank you for taking care of me."

She smiled. "Someone has to. You're a mess, girl!"

A few moments later, I braved looking at my reflection. It wasn't half bad for having a two-inch burn across my head, one eyebrow, and a blue tongue. It was what you'd call a "good conversation starter."

Randi fetched a packet of burn cream and slathered it across my head. "Lucky we didn't use it all on the lip gloss, huh?"

"Oh, our gloss! That'll cheer me up."

As we scuttled to the kitchen, I thought, *Randi's right, brows grow back in a few days, makeup covers burn scabs, and what good were bangs if you couldn't depend on them to camouflage hacked off brows? Lesson learned; always pluck unless you're trained in waxing!*

She handed me a container from the fridge. "The color's not bad, huh?"

I sniffed. "It smells funny." That was putting it mildly, this "gloss" and rotten chili could be twins. I dabbed a little on, rubbed my lips together, and spread it around.

Randi did the same. It looked like she was wearing barbecue sauce. She made a face. "It has a peppery taste."

My lips felt hot, like I'd kissed a spoonful of hot sauce.

Randi grabbed a tissue and wiped hers off. "Do your lips tingle?"

"Yeah, like they're instantly chapped."

Either my eyes were playing mad tricks on me or her top lip was growing bigger by the second. She threw me a dishtowel, turned the spigot on, and we frantically splashed water in and around our mouths. My lips were on fire! Splash, wipe, gargle, spit, splash, wipe, gargle, spit.

She pitched the rest into the trash, grabbed two frozen juices from the freezer, and tossed one to me. "These are coming in handy tonight, that's for sure."

We sat down on the floor and pressed the cans to our lips, waiting for the stinging to subside. I said, "Maybe the paprika and the cinnamon didn't mix well or something."

She leaned her head against the wall and closed her eyes. "Or the chili powder or turmeric."

For the rest of my life I'll never forget the song that played softly from the kitchen radio as we held those cans to our mouths, wondering what went wrong. Had we remembered to switch it off earlier, we would have never been able to laugh deliriously as "Our Lips Are

Sealed" by The Go-Go's crooned from the airwaves. Funny, I hadn't heard that song in well over two years. *Synchronicity.*

Afterward, we stood in the bathroom brushing our teeth, knowing that, at least for now, our mixology days were over. It was better to leave it to the experts.

I spit a blob of toothpaste down the drain and said, "If we were a rock band we'd be the Lava-Lips."

Randi laughed. "Hey, we wanted red puckers, we got 'em."

"Then why do *your* lips look nice and plump and *mine* look like I've been hit in the face with a frying pan?"

She giggled. "Luck?"

We trudged back to her room, two worn out warriors, whose battle for beauty gave them a good, hard fight. In two days I'd chewed down two of my longest nails, lost an eyebrow, a patch of arm hair, a perfectly smooth forehead, my normal looking, pink tongue, regular sized lips, and my dream of being a famous mixologist. But I'd wear my burn cream, blue tongue, and bald brow with pride as I waved that green kitty sock in the air like a surrender flag. If we stayed up any longer, what'd be next? A paper-cut? Smashed pinky toe on the bed post? Funny bone bang off the nightstand?

I curled up with my pillow—damaged and bruised—knowing tomorrow I'd continue on in my quest for beauty, scarred but unscathed. I poked my finger into one of the many holes of my sleeping bag. Even that needed mending.

Finally, I shut my eyes, and just as I was almost asleep, Randi nudged me and whispered, "Hey... *what* book?"

A Special Visitor

*M*y eyelids fluttered open and shut as the early morning sun blasted through Randi's bedroom window, causing spots to dance behind my lids and sting my puffy eyes. I squinted Randi's way and saw she was sound asleep, snoring with her mouth half open. It was Easter! My heart pitter-pattered. I absolutely *loved* Easter. Not as much as Christmas or Halloween, but it was like, a feeling, or smell in the air I couldn't quite put my finger on. And who didn't like a break from school, chocolate bunnies, baskets full of goodies, and *spring*. Soon there'd be no more snowy mud-slush, the greenery was on its way! Even the sun seemed to be smiling today. I sat up, pulled her lace curtain aside, and wondered how it could be so sunny and snowing at the same time?

"Happy Easter, Randi-roni," I whispered.

She opened her eyes and groaned.

Once she got her bearings, we wandered sluggishly to the kitchen for bowls of cereal, feeling and looking like zombies. Last night had not been one of our better evenings, that's for sure. But what wonderful thing did I see when we got to the kitchen to help me forget all about it? Two wicker baskets filled with yellow straw, jellybeans, marshmallow bunnies, packs of lollipops, Bazooka bubble gum, Hershey Kisses, and chocolate eggs. In between the baskets sat a colorful, mixed flower bouquet and a note that read:

Girls,

Happy Easter; I hope you enjoy your baskets! The mixed arrangement is for your family, Tanya, to say thank you for inviting Randi to join in your holiday dinner. Randi, call me before you go, and if you need a ride home.

Love,
Dad

I squealed and began digging out as many red jelly beans as I could and popping them into my mouth. "Your dad is freakin' gnarly!"

Randi smiled and unwrapped a lollipop. She

seemed out of it.

"What's wrong?" I asked. She was never this quiet.

She tossed the sucker back in the basket, "My stomach feels... off, like, maybe I ate too much of that chocolate icing last night."

I felt her forehead with the back of my hand. "You think you're coming down with something? I hope it's not from that lip gloss thing." Her lips were still fire engine red, but the swelling was mostly gone.

"I probably just need more sleep or something."

After throwing on sloppy, comfortable outfits, we brought our pillows and blankets to the living room and lay around watching TV until it was time to get picked up. After the last few days, I was feeling a bit run down myself. Randi fell back to sleep, and if I hadn't woken her up around noon, she might've slept all day.

We were already outside when my mom pulled up. "Happy Easter," she sang cheerfully, as we climbed in. She saw the flowers and lit up like a Christmas tree. "Are those for me?" She inhaled the sweet, floral scent and sighed. "These are *just* lovely, thank you."

I said, "They're from Mr. G." I showed her my basket. "Isn't this cute?"

"Very." Mom twisted around in her seat and patted Randi's knee. "Please tell him thank you for me. That was very thoughtful of him. It'll make a marvelous centerpiece."

Randi said, "I will. He said stop in anytime for some bulbs or shrubs, on the house."

"Maybe I'll stop in soon and introduce myself. I saw the article in the paper, he must be thrilled at how well the store's doing."

"He is. And now that he's hired more staff he'll have some time off."

Mom smiled. "That's nice." When she pulled into the driveway, though, I saw that smile fade almost immediately.

The house smelled delicious, instantly making my mouth water, and the windows were all fogged up from her cooking. I was surprised to see our living room completely rearranged, and when I glanced at Mom she had her hand on her forehead wearing a look that said, don't ask.

I scanned the rooms for Vera.

"She's having a nap. I'll wake her in about fifteen minutes," Mom said with a tight smile. "She prefers to eat supper early in the day."

She set the bouquet in the middle of the table and each time she put her nose to it she'd smile. Right away Randi laid down on the couch with a pillow over her stomach. I told Mom she wasn't feeling too hot, so she brought her a cup of tea and an afghan. It was her belief that tea cured most everything. Ginger for this, dandelion for that, chamomile to relax, green for detox, the list went on. And honey was the healing serum that topped off her magic potion. Speaking of honey and potions...

While Mom and I filled food bowls and set the table, I told her about my weekend—the good, the bad, and the butt-ugly. By the time I'd finished telling her about the blue tongue, chili-taco lips, scorched head, sugar wax, uno-brow fiasco, she was in stitches, which got me going too. It sounded so hilarious when I said it all aloud.

She dabbed her eyes with the dishcloth and caught her breath. "Oh, Tanya, you're such a colorful, spirited girl. I hope you never change." She cracked open one of the alien looking leaves from an Aloe plant on the sill and dabbed the juice on my forehead, which had already scabbed overnight. "What *am* I going to do with you?"

Our fun was interrupted when Vera entered the room complaining, "Who can rest with all this racket? Did you take the ham out yet, or will it be too dry to swallow?"

She looked even more miserable than I remembered. I sighed. "Hi, Grandma, how are you?"

Her stony, bloodshot eyes took in my off the shoulder, Beach Bunnies sweatshirt, jean skirt, leggings, hoop earrings, bracelets, hair, and multi-colored, Easter themed, nails. Her lips quivered as she looked from me to my mother, "Well, hells bells."

Mom clapped her hands together. "So, time to eat? I'm starved."

We left Vera standing there with her mouth wide

open.

The table looked gorgeous with the new dinnerware Mom had picked up at the Kaufman's sale, the floral tablecloth, matching napkins, all the food, and mixed bouquet at the center. The cream drapes with lace panels—also from the sale—brought a light, springtime feel to the room, even though it was snowing outside. I could see how much effort she'd put into this. She even had a soft piano record playing. *Spring Ballads, Volume 2.* I thought it was a nice touch.

"The table looks pretty, Mom."

Vera smirked at the flowers. "Who died?"

No one spoke for about ten minutes. You could cut the tension with a Giggles Coop switchblade. When I introduced Vera to Randi all she did was eyeball her then nod snootily. Randi gave me a "don't worry about it" look as she scooped a helping of corn onto her plate. I knew she really wanted to be lying down but was toughing it out for the sake of not wanting to appear rude. We were both on our best behavior.

When Mom offered me the dish of ham, I said, "No, thank you." It wasn't that I disliked ham; it was just that every time I ate it I was parched for hours and woke up the next morning with puffy eyelids. Too salty or something.

Vera snorted. "In *my* day you didn't get a choice. You ate what you were given, or you starved."

We acted like we didn't hear the comment as we passed the bowl of gravy around. A new song began, and the contrast of the situation made me smile. Here's this peaceful piano melody, beautiful table, and the guests are either angry, under the weather, or walking on eggshells. *Just get through dinner, Tanya, it'll be over soon, and you won't have to see this witch again for another year. In fact, eat faster.*

Vera started bombarding my mother with gossipy tales about her neighbors, their kids, the ladies at Bingo, the new cashier at Food-Lot, not even bothering to ask a single thing about anyone at the table. She ripped a dinner roll in half. "Hmm, store-bought rolls, not the ones you take the time to bake from scratch." It certainly didn't stop her from wolfing it down, though.

"Anyway, so I tell the idiot broad, the coupon says it's good *through* April, not *until* April, nitwit!" She shook her head in disbelief that the cashier in training would have the audacity to make an error in *her* presence. "Did I tell you Ethel Bender's daughter is getting married this June? Guess I'll never know how that feels because you don't meet anyone that sticks. There's such a thing as being too picky, you know."

She shoveled in a spoonful of food and continued yakking, as if she couldn't cease complaining for the thirty seconds it took to chew and swallow. Her angry face and open mouth full of mashed potatoes reminded me of one of those rabid dogs from the encyclopedia foaming at the mouth, and I laughed out loud. The three of them stopped eating and stared at me.

"Do you always interrupt adults while they're

speaking?" Vera asked.

I shook my head and put away my grin. "I'm sorry."

On and on she continued with her diatribe, dominating the conversation and my mother's attention. "Did I mention Sally Millbridge, two houses down? They delivered a piece of her mail to my box mistake, so I called her and..."

Mom was nodding politely, Randi was visiting another planet in her own head, and I stared at Vera, mentally going down the checklist of rabies symptoms. Rage, agitation, anxiety—check. Aggression, irritability, bad breath—check. Foaming at the mouth—sort of. Well that explained it, Vera was rabid. I shoved a roll in my mouth to keep from cracking up at a joke I'd never in a million years be able to tell at *this* table. I wondered if she knew she shared the same traits as a rabid raccoon.

I poured myself some ginger ale and asked, "Would anyone else like some pop?"

"Pop?" Vera rolled her eyes. "It's soda," she corrected. "Is it too much to ask kids today to use proper grammar?"

"Everyone says pop around here," I said, matter of factly.

She looked as if I'd slapped her across the cheek. "We'll, don't you have quite the smart mouth, missy?"

I bit my tongue. I couldn't stomach another second. "Mom, I'm kinda full, do you mind if Randi and I head to my room? I can help clear the table when you're ready and—"

"Your plate's not clean," Vera interrupted. "You took it, you eat it."

All that was left was a couple of green beans, some gravy, and half a roll. I didn't want to cause an argument, but I truly couldn't eat another bite, especially since *she* was the one putting knots in my stomach. I looked at my mom and raised my eyebrows.

Mom said, "Go on, honey, we'll be finished soon. Mother, would you like some tea and a slice of angel food cake?"

"You're undermining me, Jacqueline. You don't get up from the table until your plate's clean. What are you teaching her?"

Randi and I sat frozen.

"I've taught her to stop eating when she's full, not make herself sick. Why does everything have to be a battle?"

Vera was furious. "Your ill-mannered daughter does whatever she wants—has too much say in things, she does. She eats whatever she pleases, wears what she pleases. For God's sake, she's wearing a crucifix around her neck as an accessory! Do you know how sacrilegious that is? You want to raise a heathen? Fine, be my guest." She tossed her napkin onto her plate. "My appetite's ruined and I've had an ulcer—"

Ill-mannered? If anyone didn't have manners it was her! *She* interrupted others, mocked, insulted, or talked down to everyone, didn't say please or thank you or appreciate *anything*—what a hypocrite! I stood up. "Come on, Randi, I'm not listening to this. And I have *no* idea what a *sack-of-lid-juice* even is." "Egad," Vera said. "The word is *sacrilegious*, Einstein. Look it up!" She looked over at my mom, who was rubbing her forehead with her eyes closed. "Who's the mother and who's the daughter in this house? Little Miss Manners runs the show, apparently."

I was shaking with fury and embarrassment as I stomped loudly up the steps as hard as I could without destroying my feet. I could hear her unloading on my mom as I slammed my bedroom door and kicked my garbage can across the room. Why was my mom putting up with that crap? Why didn't she give her a piece of her mind? Randi knocked softly, and I let her in, slamming it shut again. It sounded like a crazy house.

Vera yelled, "*That's* my granddaughter, Jacqueline? That smart-mouthed floozy you let dye her tongue blue? What's next, a tattooed cheek? Has it escaped your attention that she resembles a Liberty Avenue streetwalker with all that makeup and teased hair? She looks like she's been electrocuted."

I didn't think I looked any different than what I saw on TV, at the mall, or at school. It was 1985, not 1945, what did she think I should wear, bobby socks, poodle skirts, and pigtails?

My mother exploded. "Enough! You will *not* insult my daughter. Do you understand? Not another word!

If you can't be respectful, then you aren't welcome in *my* home!"

I silently cheered as I sat next to Randi, who lay in a fetal position, hugging a pillow. "I'm so sorry, this is really embarrassing."

"You don't have to apologize for her, Tanya. What family doesn't have at least one wacko? My Uncle Rudy ruins *every* holiday with his drama, and one year, he threw the Christmas tree out the door and kept screaming about being a black sheep while making goat noises. It was bananas. It's like holidays force people together who normally avoid each other—for good reason." She held her stomach and cringed. "I need to use the bathroom."

I followed her out and sat on the top step to hear what Mom and Vera were saying. My mom must've been clearing the table like a wild woman as dishes *clinked* and silverware *clanked* roughly into Tupperware bowls. "Mother, I've listened to you criticize me my entire life, but I will *not* allow you to do it to Tanya."

How could my own grandmother say such hateful things about me? Weren't grandmas supposed to give you cookies and tell you how loved you were? It made me nauseous to hear what she was saying about Mom being a spinster and a rebel for wanting to protect the environment, and how she was embarrassed to only have one grandchild while everyone else had dozens. Just because my mom didn't marry and have a bunch of kids didn't mean there was something wrong with her. In this day and age women could do and be *whatever* they wanted!

I listened as they went back and forth—Mom defending herself, my clothing, my creativity, and individuality, Vera saying I was a heathen with loose morals and no discipline. Did she really think I was that bad? I thought I was a pretty good person as far as people went. Was she seeing something I didn't? I was going to look up morals in the dictionary when I got a chance. Maybe I didn't have them after all.

It got quiet, and Mom came up the steps. Her face and chest were red and blotchy, and it looked like she'd been crying. "I'm sorry for all that nonsense. Your grandmother and I agree it's best she leave. She's packing now, so I'm just going to hang here until her taxi arrives. It's no use arguing with someone who's committed to misunderstanding you." We walked down the hall to my room. "Where's Randi? I'd like to apologize for this... debacle."

"She's still in the bathroom, feeling like crap."

Mom sighed. "I'm sure this commotion isn't helping." She took my hand and we sat on the bed. "The things Grandma says are... absurd. Don't you take *one* word of it inside yourself. She's set in her ways, and... still that's no excuse, I know. I've always been tolerant, but I've drawn a line in the sand—set some clear boundaries. And she's made it clear she won't be "ordered around," as she puts it, by anyone. And that's okay, that's her choice, but she won't be coming to visit anytime soon."

I felt sad for her. "I'm proud of you, Mom. It can't be easy standing up to your own mother."

She smiled. "It is when I'm standing up for my daughter."

Randi walked in then, pained and pale. The look on her face alarmed me. I patted the bed. "Here, lay down."

"What can I get you?" Mom asked. "A cool rag? Tea?"

Randi shook her head and smiled uncomfortably. I could tell she wanted to say something but was hesitant in front of my mom. "Um, Tanya, I... do you have something I can use?"

Use? At first I didn't get it, but then it hit me. The tiredness, no appetite, holding her belly... it made perfect sense. She was having her first period! It wasn't too long ago she was worried she might be an underdeveloped freak or something. That's why she'd felt whacked out all day, she was crampy!

"Eeeee!" I jumped up and hugged her. "So good ol' Aunt Flo has finally paid you a visit, eh?"

Mom said, "Oh, this is your very first... you sweet little dear, how wonderful."

Randi looked embarrassed by the attention we were giving her. I handed her a new pair of undies from my drawer and went to get her a box of super maxis to take home. When I came back she and Mom were looking through the wall calendar counting days. Randi hung on her every word as she explained about light and heavy days and how to keep track.

"Always count from the first day of your last period," Mom told her. "At about fourteen days or so should be your ovulation time. Some call it *mittelschmerz*, meaning, mid-cycle pain, so you may feel discomfort on one side. Don't be alarmed, that's just your ovary saying 'hello, I'm doing my job.'" She sounded like a doctor. "After day twenty-one your uterus prepares to shed its lining. You may be more tired or tearful than usual as your hormones fluctuate, just use that time to pamper yourself. Hot baths, tea, yoga breathing. Expect your visit between twenty-eight to thirty-three days. The first few might be irregular until your body adjusts, so keep a little date book to keep track so you know not to wear white or light-colored pants that week." She gave her a wink.

I was overjoyed my mom could be with her at this moment since hers was clear across the country. The three of us sitting there discussing what Mom would call "women's health issues" made me feel like I was part of some special club; a sisterhood that had always been and would always be.

Randi smiled, "Thank you, Ms. Sheffield."

"Call me Jackie, and you're *always* welcome. If you ever have questions or want to talk, you know where to find me."

When Randi went to use the bathroom, I heard

Vera's cab toot the horn out front. I looked out to see the cabby lifting her bags into the trunk, and her climbing into the back, not looking back even once. I actually felt sorry for her. She'd spent her life seeing only what she didn't have instead of what she did.

Tiny snowflakes sprinkled the window as I huffed a few hot breaths onto the glass. I used my finger to draw a smiley face in the frost. A frosty window for my frosty grandma.

Mom said, "Oh, I almost forgot. I think the Easter Bunny paid us a visit. Come on."

The three of us hustled downstairs, and she pulled out two baskets from her hiding spot behind the couch. "Happy Easter, bunny rabbits!"

She handed me the purple one and Randi the yellow, each stuffed with paper straw, two nail polishes, a pop music crossword puzzle, UNO cards, my favorite chocolate-covered raisins, dried apricots, cranberries, trail mix, and bubbles! The best things of all lay beneath the straw: a journal with a butterfly cover and a pack of colored pencils!

I said, "The Easter Bunny rocks!"

Randi looked as if she was about to cry. Probably hormones. She gave my mom a hug. "Thank you. Just, thank you."

"It wasn't me, it was the Easter Bunny." She giggled. "I hope you'll use your journals." She pushed dining room chairs in, stuffed her mouth full of angel food cake, and said, "Girls, I hear a kitchen cleanup calling our names."

Mom cranked up the stereo while the three of us went to work scraping plates, clearing the table, and filling Tupperware with leftovers. And this time, she put B-94 on just for us. With Mom washing dishes, Randi drying, and me putting them away, we were flying through it. Not like when I'm solo, and it takes forever. Mom fixed up a mixed food platter for Randi to take home to her dad as a thank you for the flowers.

I heard a familiar, shave and a haircut knock, then Aunt Trish's sunshiny face breezed through the kitchen door carrying a humongous fruit basket and a bottle of wine. "Happy Easter, darlings! *Comment va tout le monde?*" (How is everyone?)

She set the items on the table, hung her black trench coat over the back of the chair, gave us each a peck on the cheek, and poured herself a cup of hot tea. "My flight was delayed almost *three* hours, or I'd have been here sooner." She sighed breathlessly, all Marilyn Monroe-like, and sipped her tea. "So, what'd I miss?"

Blazy Days

The days following Easter weekend were fairly uneventful. Our tongues and lips returned to normal with no real damage, but I was self-conscious to the max about my eyebrow, constantly peering in the mirror, adjusting my bangs, and re-touching my makeup. It took about two weeks for me to be completely comfortable again. The experience, however, helped me get the hang of tweezing and I wore them thinner than ever, even receiving compliments from other girls wanting to do theirs the same way. How could I possibly admit it had started with an accidental wax-mare?

Randi had become obsessive in the mirror for her own reasons, checking and rechecking the back of herself, terrified someone might see the bulge of her maxi pad through her pants and know she was human. She began wearing oversized rock tees to cover her bum area and would rip or roll up the shirt sleeves and throw on some stylish, waist-cinching belt with matching bracelets—whipping up quite the fashionable look for herself. It didn't take long for the RGs to follow suit. The Randi-Girls were a group of sixth graders that copied everything she did, said, and wore, even imitating her New York accent to a tee. They found excuses to come up to her in the hall and ask her advice on hair, makeup, and fashion. If she wore her hair up in a banana clip with an oversized sweatshirt and torn sleeves, you could bet these four girls would show up the next day sporting that *exact* look. It was adorable!

When we returned to school, Randi and I spent most of our time in the school library finishing up the yearbook committee project. During lunch and after school, eight of us sorted through photos, matched them with events, voted on what to keep or edit, designed layouts, and on some days, walked to Fotomat and dropped off or picked up year-end rolls of film that trickled in. Any shots or information being used for the yearbook had to be turned in before May 15th, so it was a hectic time.

Report cards came out the end of April, and I was doing better than ever, with A's, B's, and one C—in gym of all things. Maybe it was because we stood around gabbing, not caring about volleyball or badminton. Didn't Miss Bane understand what getting all sweaty in the middle of the afternoon did to our hair and makeup? Didn't she care?

Once the yearbook was off to print, and with my school work up to par, I could devote all my energy toward solidifying concert plans. The next Sunday was Mother's Day, and I figured Saturday afternoon I'd go downtown for Mom's gift and pick up tickets at the same time—you know, kill two birds with one stone. Now that I thought of it, I hated that expression. What kind of psycho threw stones at defenseless little birds then made up a saying about it? Anyway, I was waiting until I had the concert tickets in hand before asking permission to go downtown, on a school night, alone. I just *knew* it was going to be no and somehow needed to make Mom understand just how much this meant to me, that I *had* to go dance to my favorite songs being sung live by the greatest pop goddess on the planet!

The plan for Saturday was to catch the 11:15-er, *dahn-tahn,* and stop at the card store for Mom's gift— an angel charm keychain with her birthstone in the center. The commercial said you could have it engraved right there for an extra four dollars and you'd also get a free mug with your purchase. Randi said she'd hook me up with some flowers and was buying her a card as well. Then, we'd scoot over to National Record Mart for our tickets and that weekend's free poster and swag-bag promotion the radio station had advertised. Stacy and Paula had bought their tickets the Monday we were all supposed to go together, so there was a good chance our seats would be far away from theirs. That was fine with me, as long as we got in.

~ * ~

Saturday morning, we got up early, caught the bus, and boogied over to Mickey D's for a hot apple pie. I couldn't wait to get to the music store. I was in such a great mood, I could barely contain my excitement. We figured we'd be at NRM the longest, so we hit the card store first and get it out of the way. The shop was jam-packed with people buying stuff for their moms too. After purchasing a bronze angel keychain with a ruby birthstone, I waited in line for nearly half an hour to have her initials engraved. It was worth it, though, I knew she'd love it. I chose a #1 Mom mug for my purchase freebie so every time she drank her tea she'd think of me. Randi didn't seem bummed out at all Mother's Day shopping, just like I didn't care about Father's Day, it really made no difference to us. I thought it was sweet she bought Mom a card with ducks on the front that said, *Happy Mother's Day to a special friend.* It meant a lot to me that the two people I adored most were close.

Finally, we made it to the music store. It was a total zoo! Techno beats thumped and pumped through the speakers as people of all ages sifted through music, be-bopped up and down the aisles, leafed through maga-zines, and shared loud, animated conversations throughout the store.

I spotted a *Rolling Stone* Magazine with Madonna on the cover and practically cartwheeled to it. "Randi, look!" There were actually two May issues, one with her and her movie co-star, and the other with just her wearing bright, red lipstick.

"Which one are you getting?" Randi asked. "If we each buy one, we can trade clips and use the pics for the pop collage."

I looked from one to the other. They were both awesome. "Um... I'll take the one with the pearls."

Randi grabbed hers and we stopped at the giveaway booth that was being hosted by some new radio station. Each promo bag had pretzels, a pen, two bumper stickers, and a bottle opener that had *Flashaz* written across it, whatever that meant. They had a giant, cardboard bin full of free posters with a two-per-person limit. We rummaged through seeing mostly bands we'd never heard of, so I just picked two I recognized, Eurythmics and Rick James. Randi chose Sheena Easton and Simple Minds.

During the eleven minute and twenty-seven second wait in line—I know because I counted—I grew more and more excited, knowing that very soon I'd be holding in my hand a piece of paper heaven. By the time we set our magazines on the counter, fists full of cash and smiles plastered to our faces, we were ready to burst.

The cashier with the purple mohawk and half-asleep expression mumbled, "Thank you for shopping at National Record Mart, will this be all for you today?" I wondered how many times he'd said that today; probably a thousand.

I said, "Nope. Two general admission seats for Civic Arena, May 28th, please." I'd save the stub for the rest of my life and maybe even frame it and —

"That event's sold out. Will this be all for you today?"

I said, "May 28th, are you sure you're looking at the right event?"

"Like I said, all sold out." He looked at a piece of paper taped to the register and said, "There's still seats available for Iron Maiden, June 6th and the Pointer Sisters, June 21st. Grateful Dead... they've been sold out, but Beach Boys and Huey Lewis will be —"

I held up my hand. "Wait, wait, stop. So, just general admission's sold out? What about other seating?"

"Nope, whole event. Sold out."

Randi groaned.

I felt the blood drain from my face. "So, you're telling me there's absolutely *no* seats whatsoever? Anywhere? Even peanut heaven?"

"Yeah, that's what I'm sayin'." He looked irritated. "Do you want the magazines or what? Line's backin' up."

I nodded and slid over a ten. "Is there another way to get tickets?"

He rang up our magazines and put the change on the top with the receipt. "Not unless you buy 'em from someone who's already got 'em. Do you want a bag?"

"No, thank you."

My over-the-moon mood sank through the floor as we sulked out the door and to the bus stop silently. Randi, who usually had a plan B *and* C for everything, was speechless. She was thinking hard, though; I knew when her gears were turning.

I said, "Well I'm not giving up. Even if I have to stand outside and beg, or sneak in, or whatever it takes." Then I remembered something. "Blaze!"

Randi sat down on the wooden bench with the graffiti all over it and opened up the bus schedule. "As in fire?"

"No, Stacy's cousin, Blaze. He gets tickets to football games and comedy events then sells them for a higher price. I'll bet he does concerts too," I said, my hope blossoming once again.

"You mean a scalper?"

"What's a scalper? I asked.

"What you just said. They buy tickets for say, twenty bucks, then resell 'em on the street for forty-five and—"

"Well there you go. I'll call Stacy and get his digits. Boom! Problem solved." A surge of happiness tingled through me.

She raised her eyebrows. "You realize that hustle's illegal, right?"

"Who cares? *We're* not selling them, he is. They can't put us in jail for acquiring tickets from our *friend*."

She laughed. "Have you ever met this dude?"

"No, but he's Stacy's cousin and *she's* our friend so it's like we're friends by proxy. Besides, once we get formally introduced we can technically call him a friend."

The bus pulled up to the curb, and we waited for everyone to get off. The second I climbed on the smell hit me—B.O. Billy! It didn't matter where you sat, the stink permeated the entire bus, you couldn't escape it, and the next one wasn't due for at least an hour. Ugh! First, no tickets, and then I had to smell *this* the whole way home? It wasn't fair. And there'd be no enjoying my magazine either, just staring out the window, taking small sips of air through my mouth, trying to stay conscious. I dropped my quarters in the slot and whispered behind me to Randi, "Take your last breaths of fresh air while you can, it's going to be a long ride."

And boy was it ever! I had to pull my shirt up over my nose and I didn't care who thought I was weird. I'll bet the other passengers wished they had the guts to do it too. I couldn't wait to get into fresh air.

As soon as I made it home I hightailed it to my room and hid Mom's gifts in my bottom dresser drawer. She was still out shopping. Good. I dove on my bed and dialed Stacy. No answer. I tried Paula's, and they were there watching *Footloose* for the ninety-ninth time.

Paula said, "Hey girl, yinz wanna hang out tonight? We're walking down to Pizza Hut; my sister's assistant manager there now."

"Who, Marybeth?" I asked.

"No, Darla, the pregnant one."

"Oh." I couldn't keep track of who's who with her sisters; there were four of them!

She said, "We can use her employee discount any time we want, and last night after closing, she cooked us an extra-large with everything on it, and we rolled silverware and napkins for her and played as many songs on the jukebox as we wanted, for free! She promised me a part-time job as soon as I turn fifteen."

That did sound pretty cool. "I can't tonight," I said. "I'm going to the orchestra with my mom. Some collection of great composers tribute thing."

"Oh, well, la-de-da," she said.

I giggled. "It's Mother's Day weekend, shouldn't we do something *she* likes?"

Paula said, "Yeah, yeah, I got my mum a plastic rose from the 7-Eleven and a scratch-off ticket— she's lucky she's gettin' that, the wicked witch. Anyway, you get your tickets today? Where're your seats? We're like, twenty rows back from the stage, right-center."

"Well, that's kinda why I called. It's sold out. I know Stacy's cousin, Blaze, can get—"

"Say no more, hold on." She handed Stacy the

phone. "They didn't get tickets," she whispered.

"Psyche! Tell me you're kidding." Stacy said.

"Seriously, I'm wiggin' out. What about your cousin? Does he still do the ticket stuff?"

"As far as I know. Here, write this number down. Make *sure* you tell him it was me who gave it to you or he might think you're a rat or a cop or something. He's *real* paranoid. Okay, ready? It's 555-0902."

I scribbled it on the inside of my journal cover next to Jay's.

She said, "I'd call myself, but my parents will blow their stack if they find out, and I ain't gettin' grounded so close to the concert. They think he's *real* trouble. I'm not even allowed to talk to him until he 'straightens out his life.'"

"Do you think he'll have tickets?" I asked.

"Totally. He has 'em for every event except for things that don't sell out, like the circus or Pirate games. But they're way, way more expensive this way. It's gonna cost ya. If you don't get ahold of him right away, keep trying, he's always on the move."

"Stacy, I wish I could hug you through this phone. Thank you so much, I owe you *big* time."

"No problem, babe. I'm gonna finish the rest of this movie. Good luck!"

I dialed his number, rehearsing what I'd say in my head. The line was busy. I called Randi and told her what Stacy had said and that I'd keep trying until I got him. I tried a few more times before we left for the symphony, but it rang and rang. Man, I wish they made little phones you could just carry around in your pocket everywhere; things would be so much easier. Maybe like, in the year 2085.

~ * ~

The evening turned out much better than I'd expected. Heinz Hall was decorated beautifully, as usual, and the orchestra was perfection, so I felt like a jerk for sleeping through the first half. In my defense, I had been up early that day tooling around downtown, and Heinz Hall was dimly lit, cozy and warm, and the music was mega relaxing. You may as well have swaddled me in a blanket, given me a glass of warm milk, and sang me a lullaby. How could I *not* fall asleep?

Mom woke me at intermission and asked if I'd like to come with her to ladies' room. The sudden bright lights made me see spots. "No, go on, I'll wait here." I yawned and stood up to stretch my legs. When I did, I spotted an extraordinarily tall girl walking down the aisle on the tier below me. She was wearing a red, ankle-length skirt, and her bright, blonde hair stuck out like a sore thumb. Robin Garrick!

Her parents and Jay sat to her left; she had the aisle seat. I would've never guessed they were classical music aficionados. Jay was wearing a turquoise sweater, but I couldn't see his pants or shoes while he was seated. I was certainly wide awake now! I watched them for a few minutes and then the intermission chimes rang. Mom made it back just as the lights dimmed and the music began. The music sounded different now, as if Jay being under the same roof, listening to the same melody made the song a thousand times more interesting. Was he bored out of his skull? Thinking of baseball? I could barely make out the back of his head now, as he'd sunk further down in his seat and we were a whole tier behind. Just knowing he was there made me happy.

I leaned over and whispered, "What song is this?"

Mom whispered back, "'An American in Paris.' Lovely, isn't it?"

"Mm-hmm." I closed my eyes and allowed myself to sink into the song. It was easy to imagine Jay dressed in a tuxedo, twirling me under a moonlit sky. He'd kiss my satin-gloved hand, and we'd dance cheek to cheek as shooting stars whooshed above. The music went on and on, and so did my imagination. Jay and I went everywhere: to a café in Paris, where we shared kisses and a croissant; to Venice, where we ate strawberries and clinked champagne glasses in a gondola then walked hand in hand on the beach at sunset; and, finally, we ended up simply sitting on my living room floor playing cards and watching a spooky movie.

Later, as we walked to the car, Mom said, "You must've really enjoyed the performance, you stayed awake the whole second half."

I smiled. "Yeah, this was definitely the best one so far." I couldn't wait to tell Randi; she was going to freak.

The next morning, I made sure I was up by eight, so I could surprise my mom with a Mother's Day breakfast feast. She usually got up around nine on weekends, so I had an hour to whip up a veggie omelet with toast, turkey bacon, chopped fruit, and green tea with honey. I positioned her gifts on the dining room table nicely and got to work. The first omelet was too runny — too much milk, I think. The second one burned to a crisp on the bottom and was slimy and raw in the middle. The third attempt worked like a charm. I think it was because I left the lid on while it simmered on the lowest setting *before* adding the chopped veggies. Once it seemed firm enough, I flipped one side over so it looked like a burrito, and bam! Edibility.

I set the table, put on the tea kettle, and went upstairs to wake her. She was already in the bathroom brushing her teeth. "Happy mummy's day to the best mum in the universe!" I called through the door. "Come see what I made for you!"

The doorbell chimed. On a Sunday before nine? This better be good. I ran down the stairs and peeked out the window to see some dude standing there holding flowers. "Can I help you?" I asked through the glass.

"Delivery for Jacqueline Sheffield."

I unlocked both doors and took the basket. "Thank you."

"Sign here, please." He smelled like cigarettes and stinky cologne.

I used my free hand to grab the pen attached to the clipboard and scribble a squiggly line that spelled nothing. Just as it popped in my head to ask him if people tipped flower guys like they do pizza guys, he was already racing down the steps, tripping on the last one. He looked around to see if anyone saw it. The vehicle was loaded from front to back with plants and flowers, and I wondered if this was his first delivery of the day. I heard the tea kettle whistle as he screeched off like a bat out of hell. A *rabid* bat. I shivered.

"Who was that at the door?" Mom asked, tying her robe belt around her waist.

"Looky, flowers!"

I tore open the envelope as she palmed the delicate buds like tiny babies. The mixed arrangement also came with a packet of wildflower seed and green ivy filler with decorative ribbons woven throughout. I recognized the card Randi had bought yesterday.
Inside she'd written:

Happy Mother's Day, Jackie!

Thank you for your friendship and for raising an amazing daughter (my best friend). You rock!

Love,
The Gattanos

She read over my shoulder and said, "How thoughtful! I just... this is... well, I'm going to deliver a thank you card personally to them this week."

She walked into the dining room and saw the food and gifts on the table. "Tanya! You did all this?" She squeezed me to her. "I thought I smelled something delicious cooking." She winked, and I laughed because I knew it was probably the smell of the charred eggs and toast that woke her. It was no secret around here I was a horrible cook. "You're an incredible young lady, you know that?" She set the flowers down and nibbled an orange slice. She was positively glowing!

"Welp, dig in!" I told her. "A cold omelet is a rubbery omelet."

She saluted. "Yes, ma'am."

She opened her gifts while we ate and was blown away by the bronze keychain. She ran her fingers over her initials and the ruby. "This is exquisite, honey. I love it, thank you. It'll be on my keys for eternity!" She held up her #1 Mom mug and shook her head. "This is really something."

"Well you deserve it." I beamed, enjoying the fact that she looked so happy *and* that I'd successfully cooked something edible.

I refused to let her help with the dishes, so she went to soak in a bubble bath with her book, *Flowers in the Attic.*

I dialed the store. "Gattano's Nursery. Rosa speaking, how may I help you?"

"Hi, is Randi there?"

"She's with a customer at the moment, may I take a message?"

"Is Mr. G. available?"

"Sorry, he's outside loading deliveries."

"Please tell them Tanya called, and Jackie *loves* the flowers."

"Will do," she said cheerfully. "Have a nice day."

I dialed Blaze. Another busy signal, big surprise. I called every hour until I went to bed, but it was either busy or no answer. Did the dude just come home, use the phone, and leave again? Oh, well, we still had two whole weeks to score tickets. He was bound to answer sometime.

Or so I thought.

The Final Countdown - Part One

Wednesday, May 22nd...

The days flew by and still I hadn't gotten in touch with the infamous and elusive Blaze. It was always the same, either a busy signal or it rang off the hook. No one *ever* answered. Did he live alone? Have a private line in his own bedroom? There wasn't even an answering machine recording to say "Hey, you've reached *555-this sucks*. Sorry I can't take your call right now so we can discuss secret, shady, and possibly illegal deals. Leave a cryptic message and a number after the fart (fart noise) and have a sunshiny day!"

Stacy reassured me time and again that, yes, 1000% it's the right number and that he's just on the go *all the time*, be patient. That was easy for her to say, she already had tickets!

In my overly analytical brain's effort to solve this dilemma, I could think of nothing else. No matter what I was doing—eating, homework, walking to school, cutting my toenails, or plucking my eyebrows—my mind drifted to the one person that possibly held in his possession what I wanted most. I felt desperate, antsy, obsessed—I like to say hyper-focused, rather than obsessed, but it's all the same, right?

While Mrs. Phipps passionately explained the differences between active and dormant volcanoes, I gnawed my pencil like a beaver and doodled a sweet poem.

There once was a scalper named Blaze
I'd been chasing around for days
Find him I must, or I'm going to bust
Then it's hell I'm going to raise

This was getting serious. I had to formulate my next move. *What's the obstacle, Tanya?* The telephone thing. I couldn't fully relax until I'd gotten ahold of him, we only had six days left! Dealing with my mom wouldn't be easy, but it was doable. But when ya had no tickets, ya had no tickets. That had to be worked out first and foremost. I had to find him in person—his address, where he hung out. If I couldn't reach him by phone, what choice did I have? What would I do when I found his house? I'd cross that bridge when I got there. I'd ask Stacy, very nonchalantly, of course, for his last name so I could look the address up in the phone book.

So far, nothing had gone as planned. I could sit and waste my time on the what ifs and if onlys, but what good would it do? *If only* I hadn't waxed off my eyebrow and bought tickets that Monday with the girls. *If only* we'd tried harder to win them and been caller ten. It didn't matter now, we hadn't won them, couldn't buy them, and I didn't have permission to go.

Was I going to allow these ridiculously minor, gnat-like obstacles to stand in the way of something I truly wanted? Nope. Nope. Nope. To give up on something because it was challenging was to give up on your dreams. This wasn't just about tickets anymore. No, I was mad. I'd prove to myself I was willing to go the distance, no matter what it took. That's what separated the exceptional from the mediocre; the minors from the all-stars; the kittens from the tigers—you get the drift. I wasn't going to just throw my hands in the air like, oh, well, the odds weren't in my favor, maybe another time, another place, another day. No way! When an actress goes to an audition, and they say no, sorry, you're too blonde, too thin, too fat, next, does the ambitious starlet say this isn't for me, no one likes me, I stink? No, she throws her middle finger in the air and says I'm doin' it anyway, my way, like me or not!

MALL HAIR MALADIES

Things in life were going to be challenging, and if you wanted something bad enough, you had to slay those dragons with your inner sword.

My determined thoughts were interrupted by the bell, and I suddenly realized I'd gnawed my pencil down to a thin nub.

I told Randi my plan as we walked out of the gymnasium doors and down the block. She hated it. I said, "Well, smarty pants, if you come up with a better idea, I'm all ears." She just shook her head. Who was she kidding? I knew she'd be right beside me stalking the dude's house. She wanted this as much as I did, she wasn't fooling anyone with her skeptical look.

That night I called Stacy to get the scoop on Blaze, but someone was on the phone *all* night. Gawd, I was starting to despise busy signals! They even sounded evil, *neep, neep, neep.* I tried the phantom, Blaze, every fifteen minutes with no success. I kept the radio on, hoping for a miracle giveaway but it was Winning-Wheels-Wednesday. I didn't need roller skating passes, I needed concert tickets! There'd be no chance tomorrow either, it was Thirsty-Thursday, and all they gave out were cases of pop or beer. I wanted to scream!

I needed guidance. I took out every magazine I had for the month of April and read over the horoscopes. They were all pretty much the same. Sun in Aries... watch that temper... blah, blah, blah. Then I remembered, I had a *real* oracle I hadn't picked up, in like, three years. Magic 8 Ball! I flung open my closet door and scavenged through old shoe boxes, clothes, out-dated magazines—*maybe I'm a hoarder. Where are you, Magic 8 Ball, when I need you?* Aha! I found it inside a Christmas stocking I had hung on a hook.

I shook it frantically, concentrating on my questions and syncing our energies together. I asked, "Will I get in touch with Blaze before the concert?" I waited for the blue ink to settle and reveal its answer.

"Don't count on it."

What! I shook it again. "Will I go to the concert?"

"It is decidedly so."

Okay, I could work with that. "Will I get the tickets from Blaze?"

"My sources say no."

I sighed, not knowing what to think, and dusted it off with a Kleenex before asking one more very important thing. "Will I kiss a boy this year?"

"Without a doubt."

Hmm, we'll see, Magic 8 Ball, we'll see.

Thursday, May 23rd...

Five days before the concert, and the girls' room lunch crowd was buzzing with pre-concert excitement. Who was wearing what, riding with whom, and possible set lists. Some girls even made a pact to sport a fake mole above their lips for the night. Randi and I were literally the only two in that girls' room without tickets.

Monday and Tuesday were teacher in-service days—whatever that was—so students had no school. But Tuesday, concert night, *was* a school night. I thought it was so stupid for the Civic Arena to hold concerts on weekdays. They should save all the boring stuff for weekdays and the cool stuff for weekends so *everyone* could enjoy. That's definitely one for the suggestion box.

I looked around for Stacy and found her sitting in the last stall, on the toilet lid, counting out exactly five cigarettes as Paula took a seventh grader's five dimes. Stacy said, "Tell your little friends if they want 'em, they can only go through you. I can't keep having kids comin' up to me in the hall or blabbin' about it. Generics are a dime a piece, but I gotta charge fifteen cents for name brands—cost me more. Good smokes don't grow on trees, you know."

I shook my head. "Girl, you're *always* on the hustle."

She smiled. "How do you think I got the money for tickets? Think my mom was gonna spring for 'em? Thank God my whole family's a bunch of chain smokers and doesn't count the packs in their cartons."

I laughed. "Oh, yes, a chain-smoking family—total gift from God."

Randi peeked her head into the stall. "I'm outta

hairspray, can I borrow yours?"

I handed her the mini can that fits snuggly in my purse. "Be easy on it, I only have a couple sprays left, and my hair's not as stiff as it should be."

Stacy lit up a cigarette. "Did you get ahold of Blaze?"

"Oh, the phantom? No! Stacy, I'm wigging out! What am I gonna do?" I whined.

"Keep trying. You might have to catch him outside the arena."

The warning bell rang. Girls sprayed their last sprays, flushed their smokes, and scurried out the door. Paula and Randi stayed at the mirror chatting about the difference between spiral perms and body waves. "It's all in the curlers, babe," Randi told her, as she teased the back of Paula's hair and sprayed.

I wanted the scoop on Blaze, even if I had to be late for class. "Well, what's he look like?"

She took a drag of her ciggy and let it dangle between her lips as she counted dimes. "Um... tall, skinny, slicked-back ponytail, goatee. Picture a human daddy long-legger spider or a praying mantis."

I didn't want to come right out and ask where he lived, she'd never want me just showing up at his house, so I used some mind trickery. I wished I had a truth lasso like Wonder Woman. "Oh, yeah? I think I've seen that guy around. Is he the dude that lives next to the Little League field?"

"Nah, he's shacked up with some psycho broad in

the apartment next to the laundromat on the boulevard."

It worked, and I knew exactly where it was!

She bent down to readjust her black nylons. "Damn! Is it too much to ask that I make it through one day without a freakin' runner? You have any clear nail polish on you?"

I took out my makeup bag and gave her the bottle. She handed me her cigarette to hold.

"Just throw in the toilet," I said.

"I just lit it. It's only two seconds till I apply this, jeez."

"Can't you just lay it across the toilet paper dispenser?"

"Then put it back in my mouth? That's grody, Tanya. Massive poop an' pee germs."

"Oh, all right. Hurry up, we're already late." I pinched it between my fingers and held it far away from my face, lightly blowing the smoke in the other direction. Why anyone smoked those foul things was beyond me. Did boys like to kiss girls that smelled like ashtrays? I once saw a poster with a pair of black lungs with the caption; this is what happens when you smoke. That image was instantly burned into my brain forever. I'll bet her lungs will look like that one day if she keeps puffing on sicky sticks.

I dug around in my purse with my free hand for one of those nice smelling Avon lotion samples to use after I washed the stink off my fingers. The late bell rang, and I was so distracted digging for cream I didn't notice Mrs. Miller glaring angrily behind me, arms crossed, tapping her foot.

"I do hope you're enjoying your cigarette break, Miss Sheffield. Now I know where all the smoke's coming from."

Was she crazy enough to think this massive cloud of bathroom smoke had come from one little cigarette? Stacy dashed out the door. Scoundrel!

Mrs. Miller plucked the cigarette from my fingers and flushed it down the commode. "I'm disappointed, Tanya. Meet me in my office."

Randi said, "Mrs. Miller, Tanya does *not* smoke."

"*You're* late. Get to class, Miss Gattano." When Randi didn't move she yelled, "Now!"

She gave me an "I'm sorry" look before sulking out the door.

"Mrs. Miller, this isn't mine," I said. "I don't believe in smoking. Really, it's not what it looks like and—"

"Oh? Then who else was standing before me holding that smoldering stick?"

"I was just... me."

She pointed toward the door.

"Yes, ma'am." I'd been caught red-handed holding a lit cigarette. There was no excuse; even if I hadn't been smoking it, nothing would change that fact.

I started down the hall toward Mrs. Miller's office. Randi peeked out from behind the lockers and whispered, "I'll be your witness, Tanya. I'll tell her you've never smoked a day in your life. She'll *have* to let you go."

I knew better. "It doesn't matter what we tell her, Randi, she saw me holding it. She'll call my mom either way. And I can forget about going anywhere this weekend or the concert. I'll be grounded for sure. You should get to class."

She checked her watch. "Meet me on the entrance steps after the dismissal bell. Good luck."

I waited anxiously on the metal chair outside the office, wondering if Mrs. Miller had already called my mom. What would Mom say? Would she think I was a smoker? And would she believe me later when I told her honestly that I wasn't?

Mrs. Miller finally emerged from her doom-room with two boys in tow, each holding a detention slip as she bawled them out for throwing food. She called me in next. It looked exactly the same as last year when I got detention for having six consecutive tardies for health class. There'd been no good excuse, I'd been loafing in the bathroom. But *this* was major—and indefensible.

Mrs. Miller went over to the water cooler and guzzled back two paper cones full of water before sitting down and unwrapping a cough drop. She coughed into a tissue and croaked hoarsely, "Smoking on school property is a serious violation and an automatic suspension."

Suspension! "Can't I have, like, a full week's detention?"

She ignored my question as she took out a very formal looking yellow form and began writing. "You all want to grow up so quickly and destroy your health before it's time." She shook her head and opened a file with my home address, phone number, and vaccine records. I wondered what else was in there. She dialed my house on her speaker phone as I sat with fingers crossed under my legs, hoping my mom hadn't come home early like she sometimes did. I prayed while it rang and rang and tried to mask my relief when she didn't pick up.

She hung up. "Is there a work number or alternate line where I can reach your mom or dad?"

Yep! And it's locked safely in my mental rolodex.

"Sorry, no, that's the only number we have," I said, wearing my best, regretfully sorry, frowny face. I knew my mom was at work, but I wasn't telling *her* that!

She sighed and handed me the paper. "Your suspension starts tomorrow, the 24th, and since there's no school Monday or Tuesday, a parent will need to sign this verifying they're aware of this incident before you can come back on Wednesday, the 29th." She tried calling once more before dismissing me. "And next time I catch you it'll be a three-day vacation. Do you have anything to say?"

I shook my head. There was nothing *to* say. I certainly wasn't going to apologize for something I didn't do. I held onto the hope Stacy would burst in, admit the cigarette had been hers, and save me, but she didn't. I was really going to give it to her when I saw her!

As I stood up to leave she rolled open her bottom desk drawer to retrieve another cough drop from her purse, and, when she did, what did I see? A pack of menthol 100s and a Zippo lighter in the side pocket!

I walked down the hall fuming. People were such hypocrites! "Friends" let you take the fall for their crimes, grandmothers attacked your manners while having none themselves, and principals punished you for doing the same things they did!

I moped in the bathroom stall, reading graffiti until the bell. I was half tempted to take out a pen and unleash a creative combo of words myself but, with my luck, I'd get caught and be accused of having been the blue marker bandit all along and have *another* suspension!

As Randi and I walked down the front steps she handed me a note from the weasel. "Paula and Stacy snuck home while you were in the office. Stacy couldn't face you. She's really upset, Tanya, she knows it was a scuzzy thing to do."

"Whatever." I opened the origami folded note. "If the weasel was really sorry she'd have come to the office and 'fessed up!"

KRISTY JO VOLCHKO

Tanya,

Pleeeeeeeez forgive me. I'm sorry from the bottom of my heart. I froze! If I get one more suspension, I'll be grounded the entire summer! Thank you for not ratting me out. I swear I'll make this up to you somehow. I made a stupid mistake, please don't hate me! I couldn't bear to lose your friendship.

Stacy

I crumbled it into a ball and threw it in the trash can by the fence. Friends didn't let you take the heat for something *they* did! But Stacy had been this way since kindergarten, probably always would be, and I always forgave her. She smoked, cut school, swore like a trucker, snuck out, and hustled cigarettes. She was a sneaky little devil, the first to snag an extra donut from the snack bin or steal a jump rope from the gym box. I expected nothing less. Who knows? Maybe that's why I hung out with her. She was wickedly entertaining and the devil on my shoulder. She also did some adorably thoughtful things that made me forget her behavior—until the next time. Somewhere deep down I know someday she'll go too far.

"Are you gonna tell Jackie?"

"Are you kidding? She'll have a cow. No way. And I'm gonna have to turn the ringers off for the next couple of days in case Mrs. Miller tries calling my house again." I didn't know what she'd say, but I knew it wouldn't be, *oh, you're suspended? Have a great time at the concert!* In this case, what she didn't know wouldn't hurt her. Personally, I thought it was unhealthy to tell your parents everything, and I wanted to lead a healthy lifestyle. I mean, shouldn't you have your own life? Your own secrets? Did parents need to know every single thing about you?

I said, "Since I have to pretend I'm at school tomorrow, I'm gonna use the time to find Blaze's house and knock on the door." I fully expected Randi to object, but she smiled. "I'll cut tomorrow. I've only missed four days of school the entire year, and we only have three weeks left till graduation. Why not?"

I jumped up and down. "I love you! You know I'd never ask you to do that for me, but we're going to have the best day *ever!*"

Now that I had a description of what he looked like and where he lived, things were looking up. And I could get away with not telling my mom about the suspension by simply signing the paper myself to give to Mrs. Miller on Wednesday. I wasn't thrilled with what had happened today, but I had to admit there was a silver lining in all this. I was going to link up with Blaze and score us some tickets!

That night, I snuck around and turned the ringers off on all three phones, signed my mother's name to my suspension slip, and shoved it between the pages of my science book. Phone tampering, forgery, suspension. Was it really as awful as it sounded? But I wasn't even smoking! It wasn't fair to get in trouble for something I didn't do. It was easy to avoid my mom that evening because she'd been working nonstop on some work project for days now and was buried in paperwork.

Before I went to bed I tried the phantom, still no answer, then I called Randi to go over a solid plan for the morning.

"Stacy's been trying to call you all night to apologize," Randi said.

I whispered, "Whoop-de-do. Did you mention that her disgusting smoking habit and rat-like behavior is the reason my ringer's off?"

"No, I just said I'd tell you."

I said, "Anyway, I'll meet you at T's Diner on the boulevard at 8:15, and don't forget to bring your loot. After we link up with Blaze we can goof off, go shopping or something."

"Okey-dokey, smoky."

"Did you just call me *smoky*?"

She cackled. "Oh, wait, was it too soon? I didn't mean it. I swear."

"Yeah, yeah. Nighty-night."

She said, "Nighty-night, sleep tight, don't let the bed bugs bite, and while you're there, kiss a bear, and don't forget your underwear-"

"Stop!" I giggled. "You're *so* outer limits, I swear.

Goodnight!" I hung up the phone and smiled. She was so silly.

The plan was easy. We'd get up for school like always, but instead of walking to Seaton, we'd walk up the boulevard, knock on Blaze's door, and ask for some made up name, like we'd knocked at the wrong house. I'd say, "Hi, is Jane Smith around?" He'd say, "Sorry, wrong place." I'd go, "Oh, sorry about that. Say, you look really familiar, like my friend Stacy's cousin, what a small world!" He'd say, "Yeah, that's me." We'd get to talking, I'd mention the arena, he'd offer tickets, and we'd have the rest of the day to blow off. Sounded like a great day to me. Being suspended was like having a vacation day! Schools seriously needed to rethink their method of consequences.

~ * ~

Friday, May 24th...

The next morning, we sat inside a booth at T's Diner sipping hot cocoa with mini marshmallows floating on the top, staring across the street at Blaze's apartment building. We could officially add stalking to our growing list of crimes, right under truancy, smoking, corruption, lying, school suspension, forgery, and phone tampering. Hopefully, I could soon add purchasing unauthorized tickets. Maybe Vera had been right all along, maybe I was a heathen.

As I silently prayed that neither of our parents decided to stop in there for a meal, Randi popped a bubble and read her Bazooka comic. "Ha! Listen to this, 'You will be a fine swimmer and make the Olympic team.' Stupidest fortune ever."

I squeezed mine in my hand and closed my eyes. "Whatever this says will be my fate with this concert." I read, "'Even a broken clock is right twice a day.' What does that mean? Are we getting tickets or not? The oracle ball said we are."

"What oracle ball?"

"Magic 8 Ball. It said we'd get tickets."

"Oh, cool." Randi slid over a dime. "Try calling him again before we go over."

I scooted out of the booth and used the pay phone to dial the number I knew by heart. I plopped back into my seat. "It's busy," I said, guzzling the rest of my lukewarm cocoa. "That means he's home. Don't take your eyes off that door in case he leaves."

I paid the check as Randi watched the door, then we crossed the boulevard to the shabby, two-story duplex, and rehearsed our story. When we stepped through the main door into the entry hall Randi actually gagged. The smell of cat pee was overwhelming. Half of the green carpeting was all ripped up like a dog had chewed it apart—exposing moldy, rotted wooden planks underneath. Paint peeled down the walls, and dead centipedes, potato bugs, and spider carcasses floated from webs in every corner. There was a rusty, ten-speed bicycle with a flat tire chained to the railing with a pair of extremely worn sneakers dangling from the seat by their laces. I said, "I can't take this smell."

Randi held her nose. "I know. This is foul, let's hurry."

There were two doorbells—one missing a label, an intercom, and another security door. We'd have to be buzzed in. Cripes!

"How do we know which one it is?"

I said, "I don't know. We'll ring both."

"Good idea," she said, jabbing the buzzer for 101— Bertha Yakliv. She whispered, "You *know* that can't be his girlfriend's name, she sounds a hundred years old."

"Yeello!" screeched the elderly voice from the intercom.

I said, "Um... hi."

"Whooo is it?"

"It's... uh, Tanya."

"Speak up, I can't hear you!"

"Tanya!"

"Tanya don't live here!" *Click.*

Randi giggled. "Why is she yelling at us?"

"Probably can't hear good," I said. I pressed 201 two or three times. "Someone has to be home. The line was busy."

Randi said, "Maybe he's sleeping, and his phone's off the hook so he doesn't get woken up with calls."

I looked around. "Every building has a couple of entrances. Let's go around back, maybe it's unlocked."

We walked between the buildings to the back alley and knocked on the gray, metal door with the missing handle. Randi saw me staring at the metal fire escape leading up to the apartments and said, "Oh, no. Don't even think about it."

I laughed. "What?" I grabbed a handful of gravel and ducked behind a blue dumpster. "I'm gonna toss a few pebbles up to the second-floor window, tell me if a face looks out."

Randi ducked down next to me. "If you're throwing rocks, I'm hiding too."

"I'm not throwing rocks, I'm tossing pebbles."

"What's the difference?" she asked.

"It's just... stop distracting me and keep watch."

I looked around nervously then flung a couple small stones at the window with the ratty blind. They were too light to make it up that high, so I tried some slightly bigger ones, and they made contact everywhere *but* the window. *Plink! Plunk! Plink!*

"No one's looking out," Randi reported, grabbing a handful of gravel. She picked out a stone, tossed it up, and it pinged off the railing. The next she chose looked a bit on the larger side, and, after she threw it, I heard a crisp, cracking sound. I looked up, and sure enough, the glass had spider cracks throughout.

I gasped. "You cracked the freakin' window!"

Randi said, "I didn't mean to! The rock wasn't

even that big!"

We took off running up the alley and didn't stop until we reached the end of the boulevard. I'm no lawyer but I was pretty sure we could add criminal mischief, trespassing, and vandalism to the week's list of accidental crimes.

"I seriously didn't mean to do that." She looked like she was about to cry. "Do you think someone saw us? Should I leave a note and some money?"

"We can't show our faces there now," I panted. "We can't go back." I kept looking behind us to see if anyone was following. "I have no idea how much a window costs, but it wasn't shattered, just cracked. Maybe they can just put some duct tape on it or something."

"I feel terrible. I didn't even throw that hard. You saw how easy I was throwing, right?"

I said, "I feel bad too, Bionic Woman, believe me, and we don't even know for sure whose window that was. But if we go back, they might call the cops, and I'm not in the mood to go to jail today. We'll have a police record, too, and then we can forget about getting into college and our futures. There's no way we'll make it to Mexico with twenty dollars each."

She looked terrified. "What? What are you talking about? I don't want to go to Mexico!"

"I'm just sayin' I'm not going back, and we should thank God it didn't bust out the whole window. They may not even notice it. Let 'em think a bird flew into it or something. It's more common than you think, you know. It happened to my Uncle Doug's bathroom window while he was on the crapper."

Randi laughed. "No way!"

"Yep, bird flew right into it. Broke the window and itself. True story. Accidents happen, Randi, you didn't do it on purpose."

She opened a piece of gum and shook her head. "This is bad, bad karma, man."

"I agree," I said. "It's not cool to just leave it like that. I don't want yucky karmas either. So, look, we'll put our next two allowances together, write an anonymous note, and stick $25 in their mail slot. That'll cover at least some of it. It's just glass. I mean, how much can a piece of glass be?"

She smiled. "I like it. Sounds like a good deal. I feel, like, a hundred percent better knowing were gonna square up."

I looked at my watch. "We still have a few hours till school lets out. Watcha wanna do?"

She said, "I'm starving. Let's take the back streets to Mickey D's. I don't want to get spotted by anyone."

"Cool beans. And I'll keep trying to call the phantom. We can still reach him before Tuesday, I have a good feeling about it."

At Mickey D's, we ate our cheeseburgers and fries at the most inconspicuous booth we could find—back by the bathrooms—and read our horoscopes from a left-behind newspaper.

MALL HAIR MALADIES

May 24, Scorpio: Today will be driven by intensity from start to finish. Stick to clear paths and procedures as there is a tendency to misjudge finances and matters of the heart. Lucky numbers: 7, 4, 3, 19. Color: Blue.

It made perfect sense! Seven was what time I'd gotten up that morning, four was how many days were left until the concert, three was how many weeks we had until school ended, nineteen was how many bottles of nail polish I had in my collection, and I was wearing blue jeans today. Bam! There was no denying these horoscope writers were true seers.

Randi was quiet, not caring much about her horoscope, still upset about the window and worried about karma. I bought her an apple pie and reminded her we'd be sending money and a note to the window victims. Karma cleared. I know I felt better.

That night, neither of us was much in the mood for a sleepover. What I really wanted was a hot bubble bath and some alone time to recharge my batteries, and that's exactly what I did. I ran myself a bath, sprinkled in some chamomile and oat powder my mom had bought from the hippie store, leaned back, and leafed through the pages of some book about the soul's energy my mom had left on the stand.

After reading this super inspiring chapter on the importance of positive energy and the laws of attraction, I closed my eyes, inhaled the soothing aroma, and spent the next few minutes concentrating on clearing the negative energy of the last few weeks from my spirit and ushering fresh, positive vibes into my chakra centers, just like it instructed.

I envisioned holding the tickets in my hand, what they'd look like, how they'd feel. I saw Randi and me dancing to the music and singing alongside thousands of others with our arms raised in the air. I pictured all my friends and family standing in a circle singing songs as uncle Doug played the guitar. Grandma Vera was there too. She and Mom were laughing as they danced together, hand in hand. Randi, her dad, Aunt Trish, Stacy and Paula, and even Mrs. Miller stood clapping and smiling. I took all my loving thoughts for them and imagined pushing joyful energy their way. I stayed in the water so long my fingers and toes were pruned to the max, but I felt more relaxed than I had in days. I dried my hair, put on my flannel jammies, and sunk into a relaxing, peaceful sleep, accepting that a person could only do so much before they had to leave it in the hands of fate. And I knew I'd be at peace with whatever happened from here on out. Great book!

The Final Countdown - Part Two

Saturday, May 25th...

*a*fter calling the phantom all afternoon, something bizarre happened. I was so used to no one answering that I was caught off guard completely when someone picked up on the first ring.

"What!" screamed the angry woman. No hello, no beating around the bush, no niceties.

I froze.

She yelled, "What? Cat got yer tongue? Another prank call?"

I cleared my throat. "Um... hi, is Blaze there?"

"And who is *this*?"

"It's Tanya, I just wanted to—"

I heard a thud as she ranted, "It's another one of your skank ho-bags calling *my* phone again, Blaze. *My* phone. You know the one you *don't* pay for? And get your stinky, rotten garbage feet off my couch! How 'bout you let *her* wash your boxers 'cuz I'm sick of it!"

Skanky ho-bag? "Excuse me, miss, it's not what you think. I'm a friend of his cousin's and—"

"Bull! I know *exactly* who this is and if I ever see you in my bar again I'm gonna snatch you off that bar stool by your greasy hair and—"

Who did she think I was? I'd never been inside a bar in my entire life! And my hair was *far* from greasy.

Blaze got on the phone and grumbled, "Yeah?"

"Hi, is this Blaze?" I ask politely.

"Who-ziss?"

"I'm a friend of Stacy's and—"

"Why you callin' me at this number?"

He wouldn't let me get a single sentence out! What's her face was still in the background ranting about stained boxers, beer bottles, and greasy-haired hoes.

"Tickets. I'm calling for tickets to the—"

"Oh, hey, whoa... I don't talk on the phone," he said. "Don't know what you're talkin' 'bout. Don't know nuthin' 'bout no tickets." *Click.*

Seriously? What a total schizoid! I'd been calling for weeks for *that*? That whole family was deranged! I called Randi and told her what happened.

She laughed. "Ha! Skanky ho-bag. That's hilarious. I'm glad they *didn't* answer the door now, jeez. We might've been kicked down the stairs, and you would've gotten your 'greasy' hair pulled!"

"I know, right? Now I don't feel so bad if it *was* their window, serves them right for being so nasty. Anyway, we've done all we can do for now. It's time to leave it up to the forces that be. Watcha got cookin' today?"

Randi said, "I'm gonna work at the store today, pick up some extra dough for..." she whispered, "the glass. Don't worry about covering half, I got it."

"I can't let you do that, Randi—"

"Seriously, Tanya, I got it covered. I'm the one that broke it. Luv ya. Call you tonight." She hung up before I could object again. She was a *real* friend. Not like that weasel and her crazy cousin.

~ * ~

Sunday, May 26th...

Sunday morning, my mom said she needed office supplies then was heading to Book World, and would I like to join her. Since I'd enjoyed her book on positivity so much I thought I might tag along and look for something on karma. I was really curious about this karma stuff. Was it real? Did you have to right all your wrongs or get the shaft sometime later? Was lying to your mom part of that deal? She was thrilled I'd read some of her bathroom book and spent the entire car ride filling my ears with tidbits about chakras, spirit guides, angels, moon signs, and crystals. It was a very interesting, inspiring conversation. I had no idea I had something called a rising sign ascendant and was in the first of three decans of my sign. I thought you just read your horoscope, and that was it. I wanted to learn more.

As we rode the escalator up to the second floor of Book World, she said I could pick out any two books I wanted, her treat. Nice! I browsed the young adult shelves first, finding at least three that looked good, but when I moved on to the New Age and Astrology section I was in heaven! There were so many amazing books, how could I possibly choose?

I grabbed a basket and filled it to the brim with books on ancient religion, karma, reincarnation, ghosts, angel spirit guides, God, numerology, mysteries from beyond, astronomy, and astrology. *Why weren't there any carts here?*

I dragged my hundred-pound basket to the far corner of the store where I sat cross-legged on the carpet for over an hour, skimming through each book—absorbing as much into my brain as possible. It was a daunting task trying to decide which two I absolutely couldn't live without; I wanted to devour them all. Ultimately, I ended up choosing, Linda Goodman's *Sun*

MALL HAIR MALADIES

Signs and *1985's Astrological Vibes*, which had a daily horoscope for each sign, as well as a love compatibility and numerology section. I liked that one so much I used some of my saved-up concert money to buy Randi a copy as well. She was going to love it! I also bought a pack of guardian angel tarot cards that came with a little instruction booklet. I was so excited because these were the first real astrology books I'd ever owned, and I knew I'd take excellent care of them. No stickers or doodling allowed! I'd write my name on the inside covers though, that would be okay.

Mom bought books on gemstones and crystals, daily meditation affirmations, and aura reading. I'd probably read those when she was finished, and I had a feeling I'd be taking a lot more bubble baths.

When we got home I decided to eat something healthy, like yogurt, to go with my new positive thinking regime, instead of just grabbing my usual oatmeal cookies and sweets. I curled up on my bed, ready to feast on my new reads but, instead, ended up crashing out for two hours. I woke up, wondering why I hadn't heard from Randi all day then remembered I'd shut off all the ringers. I shook off the cobwebs and rang her line.

She picked up on the first ring. "I've been calling and calling!"

"I forgot the ringers were off, what's up?"

"Oh... my... gawd! This is gonna flippn' blow

your mind to the max!"

"What!"

"Have you talked to the girls at all?" she asked.

"No, I haven't talked to anyone, I fell asleep. What's going on?"

She took a breath. "Okay, so, Paula calls super early this morning, I mean, like, butt crack of dawn early. I wanted to strangle her. Anyway, so last night, they bought those Ogilvie Home Perms so Paula's sister, Shelly, could give them spiral perms. You know, she's going to cosmetology school and all."

"Didn't they just dye their hair a few days ago?" I asked. "You're supposed to wait a week or two between."

"Right. So, Shelly tells 'em she won't do it for at *least* two weeks, and that it wasn't healthy for their hair — too harsh with the chemicals. Well, you know Stacy. You can't tell her anything. She didn't wanna wait. Even Paula was warning her not to do it, to listen to Shelly. But Stacy insisted, saying she'd do it herself then."

I groaned. "She didn't. How'd she do the curlers in the back?"

"Paula helped her with the curlers—against her better judgment. So, Stacy mixed up the neutralizer and the solution or something, leaving it on twice as long, and totally fried her hair!"

I gasped. "Shut... up! Is she bald?"

Randi said, "Not completely hairless bald, but

Paula said it was wicked dry like horses' hair or straw before it started falling out in clumps. So, Stacy's screaming hysterically, Paula's crying and gathering clumps of hair off the floor, Paula's mom was trying to calm them both down, her dad was freaking out because he's on some weird work shift and needs sleep, and Shelly's baby was screaming at the top of its lungs with a teething fever. You gotta hear Paula tell it. She said it was B-A-N-A-N-A-S."

I felt awful for all of them; the whole thing sounded horrible. If it were me, I'd be devastated. But I wouldn't go against the advice of a trained hairdresser either. Could something like this be karma for the crappy things Stacy does, like promoting smoking to little kids for a dime or letting a friend take the heat for her? Did karma work like that? It scared me to think so—I was no angel myself. "So, is she bald or what?"

"Well, Shelly had to take her to a barber friend to have it shaved. He had no choice, it was falling out."

It was every girl's worst nightmare. My waxed eyebrow and swollen lip situation seemed like small potatoes in comparison. My heart really did ache for her, even after what she'd pulled Friday. "Is she okay?"

"She was hysterical most of the night, locked herself in Paula's bathroom. Her uncle had to go over there and take the door off the hinges to get her out. It was bad—real bad. Now her hair's like Mia Farrow's from *Rosemary's Baby*. She refuses to leave her room, go to school, and won't even go to the concert. So, now Paula doesn't want to go to the concert without her."

"The tickets!" I got excited.

"Shelly already snagged 'em. I know, I was bummed."

"I wouldn't have gone without you either." I said, "You know, if I could pick one song that suits this situation exactly—"

Randi giggled. "Lemme guess, 'Almost Cut My Hair' by that one group, Crosby-Steals-Cash?"

"*Bzzzz*, guess again."

"Oh wait, 'Hair of the Dog' by Nazareth!"

"*Bzzzz*, nope."

"Okay, I give up."

I giggled. "Why, 'Karma Chameleon,' of course, darlin'."

"You're such a booger!" She laughed.

"I've been reading a lot about karma and Laws of Attraction lately... just sayin'. Speaking of which, I bought you the raddest book today—an astrology one. I'll bring it over tomorrow."

"You're so sweet, thank you!"

"I'm about to go have a chat with my mom about Tuesday night so wish me luck."

"Oh. Lemme know how it goes. I'm talkin' to my dad, too, telling him maybe Jackie can take us, but I'm not mentioning scalpers. I'm just gonna be vague."

"Kay, call you later."

I went to my desk and jotted down some key

points to mention.

- The importance of music in one's life.
- How awesome my last report card was.
- You're only young once.
- How I demonstrate mature and responsible behavior consistently. (Sans the secret lying, suspension, stalking, criminal mischief, and all the rest.)
- It's the end of the school year, I have no tests on Wednesday, and an event on a school night won't matter.
- A great source of artistic inspiration & research that will benefit my career as a photographer. See? Thinking of my future—now that's maturity!
- It's the perfect early birthday or eighth-grade graduation gift if she was thinking of getting me something. Now she could save the cash & buy herself something nice instead.
- Will be the highlight of my entire life, and I'll always be indebted to her for allowing this life-long memory to occur.

Things *not* to mention under any circumstance:

- No actual tickets—sold out.
- The word scalper.
- Alone.

- Downtown.
- Night.
- No ride home. (Haven't quite worked that part out yet since the 44S stops running at 10:15 on weeknights.)
- Cigarettes, suspensions, broken windows, principals, Blaze, or any other trigger words that might precipitate a slip of the tongue.

I read over the list once more, did a five-minute positivity meditation exercise to boost my chances of a favorable outcome, and went to knock on her bedroom door. She was sitting in a chair with her feet propped up on the bed frame surrounded by legal pads, stacks of file folders, and environmental literature on oil spills. Did she realize she had three pencils sticking out of her hair bun?

"Mom, I know you're super busy, but can I ask you something important? And can you please hear me out before you say no?"

She took off her glasses, giving me her full attention. "All right, shoot."

"So, there's this very important event I'd like to go to, and it's the most important thing of my whole life. If you say no, I'll literally keel over and die from a broken heart or, worse, a ruptured kidney or liver."

She smiled. "That important, huh? I'm sure your organs can handle—"

"No, they can't."

"Which event?"

"A music concert at the Civic Arena. Can I go?"

Mom opened her calendar. "What day is it? I'll see if I can—"

"Tuesday night."

"Two days from now? That's *really* short notice, Tanya, I have late conferences until Thursday and—"

I held up my hands. "Relax, Randi and I have it all figured out. We'll take the bus."

"How about tickets?"

"That's a very good question, Mom, and we'll find some when we get there."

"Find some? What does that mean? And I'm not comfortable with you taking a bus home that late in the evening."

"Mom, there'll be hundreds of parents everywhere, we won't be alone. And there'll be plenty of people holding ticket signs and—"

"Scalpers? Oh, no. If you can't purchase tickets from a window forget it. Also, I'll need confirmation from Randi's dad what time he'll be dropping you off *and* picking you up."

I stood up and paced the room. "I'm not a baby, Mom. I think I'm pretty responsible. I know how to get on a bus."

"Yes, Tanya, *you* are responsible and trustworthy. It's not *you* I have trust issues with. Do you know how many weirdoes are out there roaming the city streets at night? And may I ask why you're coming to me two days before the event? Surely you knew about this sooner."

"Because I knew you'd give me a hard time and I was right!"

"I'm sorry, Tanya, I'd feel more comfortable if you actually had tickets and there was an adult with you."

"But I can handle myself!" I folded my arms and glared at her accusingly. "I know what this is about. You don't like my music, you said so yourself... called it *bubble gum pop*. And I heard you telling Aunt Trish that these female pop singers were sending the wrong messages to impressionable girls, *and* you called Madonna *Ma-goon-a!*" I was really fired up now.

My mom burst out laughing. "Honey, no... I—"

"This isn't funny, Mom! You of all people know how important music is, you're *still* talking about that three-day-long hippie concert, Tweety or Woodstock or whatever it was! Well this is *my* Woodstock!" I fumed.

She stood up and started stacking papers into piles and clearing off her bed. "This is a *far* cry from Woodstock, Tanya. Those were very different times. A war was going on, and we used music to demonstrate a message of peace and unity."

"Mom, this might be a different time, but it's mine and Randi's time to enjoy the music *we* love. Millions of others love it too, you know, they can't all be wrong!"

"I understand what you're saying, Tanya, but this

isn't about the music. You *are*, in fact, thirteen years old, *not* eighteen. It'll be late when the concert lets out and—"

"Ooh!" I was so frustrated, I stormed out of her room, dove on my bed, and scribbled frantically in my new diary as the tears I'd been holding in flowed like rain.

Dear Diary,

I knew she wouldn't understand!!! I hate being thirteen! Everyone treats you like a baby and you're not old enough to do anything good, like be out late, drive, or work in a rad clothing store. But it shouldn't matter. I get good grades, never sneak out like some of my friends do, I'm always on time for curfew, I don't smoke, drink, or do drugs. I don't even eat as much candy as I used too, but nothing's ever good enough! I can't wait till I'm eighteen so I can go anywhere I want and run my own life!

I put a tape in my Walkman and closed my eyes, allowing Air Supply to cool my jets. It was my go-to relaxing music. Mom walked in and said something. I took off my headphones, but I didn't look at her.

"Can we discuss this calmly?" she asked.

I rolled onto my side, away from her. "What's there to discuss? I tried being honest and look where it got me. You think I'm too young to do anything cool and you hate my music, period."

She sat on the edge of my bed. "My issue isn't your age or your taste in music or even that it's a school night, Tanya. You girls trying to buy tickets from some stranger on the street downtown is... it's dangerous. You can't see how I'd be the least bit concerned for your safety? Look at it from my point of view."

"But Paula and Stacy go everywhere by themselves, even at night and—"

"I'm not Stacy's or Paula's parents. You have to take some responsibility in this, Tanya. You've had ample opportunity to speak to me sooner than forty-eight hours before. This was poorly planned, and now you're angry because I don't like the idea of my young daughter and her equally young friend roaming the city searching for scalpers. I'm sure this artist will tour here again."

I sat up. "You always say where there's a will there's a way, to never give up on things that mean a lot to you. Well, that's all I'm trying to do! You have no idea the amount of energy I've put into trying to make all this come together. Then I come to you hoping you'll understand, and you're not even *trying* to compromise."

Mom nodded. "That's fair. All right, here's my compromise. If, by some miracle, Randi's father can acquire tickets *and* accompany you, you can go. But I want a phone call to confirm it."

I didn't see where the compromise was in that. "But what if he can't?"

"Then you'll have to accept that. It's my final of-fer—my *only* offer." Mom kissed me on my forehead. "Are we good?"

I smiled. "We're good."

At least now I knew what her bottom line was, and she knew I wanted to go to an event that night. With a little maneuvering here, a fib or two there, I could make it work.

My whole life I'd seen my mother battle passion-ately for the things that mattered most to her—the rights of others, the environment, the things that spoke to her soul. Would she want me to be any different? I didn't think so. We weren't seeing eye to eye on this particular issue, and that was okay, I was certain we'd see differently on a lot of issues in the years to come. But when it came down to it, I'd have to decide what was best for me and my life, and this was one of those times.

It wasn't like I was asking to buy liquor and throw a party for underage kids, wanted to take a bus across the country by myself for a week, or use her credit card to redecorate my entire room—it was a concert on a school night, nothing more. Why couldn't she see that? Until recently I couldn't recall the last time I'd lied to her or gone against something she said, but in this in-stance, I truly believed she was being too strict. I was going to be fourteen in six months, couldn't she loosen the reins a little?

I was already scheming as to how this would all go down when I leaned over and clicked on the clock radio to fall asleep. "Lucky Star" was playing. *I hear you, fate, loud and clear.*

~ * ~

Monday, May 27th...

Since there wasn't any school, Randi and I decided to spend the afternoon at my house trying on outfits and finalizing plans. I could hardly believe that in just twenty-four hours we'd be enjoying the greatest night of our lives! I summarized for Randi the bogus conversation I'd had with my mom, and it was pretty much the same deal with her dad—she had to go with an adult, and *no* scalpers.

As I rooted through my closet—the abyss—in search of the perfect jacket to go with my chosen concert attire, my mind drifted off into one of my many bubble dreams.

I walk into Randi's kitchen where her dad's sitting at the table wearing a frown. "What's wrong Mr. G.?"

"Well, Tanya, my entire class has come down with a bad case of adult chickenpox—it's been going around for days. Whatever will I do with the evening?"

MALL HAIR MALADIES

I say, "I think a concert might cheer you up. We don't have tickets though."

He says, "Well, I don't mind buying them from the nice salesman holding a sign outside the arena. I'll even grab a few T-shirts and posters."

When we arrive, he hands us the tickets and says, "Girls, I'm feeling a bit under the weather; I may be coming down with this chicken bug too. I'll nap in the car until the show's over. Have fun!"

I pulled my denim jacket with the corduroy collar off the hanger and sighed. If only we were that lucky.

Tuesday, May 28th, 1985

*D*ress You Up" blared from the speakers of Randi's dining room stereo as I crammed my makeup and money into my purse. I thought of it this way: we'd be leaving them notes telling them where we'd be, and there'd be thousands of adults around, so no lying there. I'll admit, my excitement for the day was slightly deflated knowing it had come down to us leaving fib-filled notes for our parents. As much as I wished it had turned out differently, I knew some things just couldn't be helped. It was like that Naval officer chick who said something like, "Tis far easier to ask forgiveness than to get permission." I couldn't agree more.

If things went according to plan, my mom would find her sticky note on the fridge door saying I was at the concert with Randi and her dad, and Mr. G. would find his note on his desk saying Randi went with me and my mom. We'd locate a scalper the second we arrived, enjoy the concert, absorb magical, lifelong memories into our hearts and brains, and make sure we caught the last outbound 44S bus home. No harm, no foul. It was perfect!

I went over everything in my head once more as I primped in front of the mirror. I couldn't see anything jerking up the plan at this stage; I was positive we'd covered everything that could possibly come up. So why did I have the nagging feeling I'd forgotten something? My suspension day was out of the way, the paper was signed, and the ringers in both houses were turned off, so neither parent could confirm things with the other. We'd most likely run into Blaze or some other scalper outside the event, so I wasn't worried about tickets, and we were bringing all the money we'd saved until now, so we could afford the jacked-up price.

I'd given a lot of thought to this scalper business over the last few days, and if it was such a crime, why didn't the police arrest them? I honestly didn't understand what all the hullabaloo was about. I mean, isn't that what car salesman did? Grocery stores? Hot dog carts? They bought a ten pack of wieners, for, I don't know, fifty cents, and a pack of buns for fifty cents (a buck total for those who hate math), then the cart dude sells each wiener for a buck, making nine bucks profit on the deal. How come that was okay and scalping was frowned upon? Wasn't that just business? Didn't scalpers deserve to make a living too? And that scary name, *scalper*—it sounded way too axe murder-ish for my taste, like they were the type to scalp you with a hatchet. I decided to rename it something cuter like Ticket-Angel. Yes, it sounded much better to purchase a ticket from a Ticket-Angel rather than a scalper. Maybe I could do their marketing.

Anyway, I planted seeds in my mom's ears last night that I was heading to the mall for shoes and a movie and would be gone all day, acting as if the concert issue was totally squashed. Fearing she'd sense I was up to no good, I wanted to be G.-O-N-E the entire day in case she tried to pull something and come home early. The woman had an eerie witch-like intuition that I knew from experience not to underestimate. I thought the note should be short and sweet, not saying too much and leaving a little wiggle room in case things went south.

Mom,

Change of plans... at the concert with Randi and her dad. I should be home around 11-ish. I'll grab a snack. Don't worry, I'll be fine!

Love,
Me

MALL HAIR MALADIES

Around two, I called her from Randi's to tell her I was leaving for the mall, but really, I was fishing to see if she'd been home and saw my note. She sounded busy, preoccupied, and said she'd be home by 7:00 at the latest. By that time, I'd be long gone and walking through the arena doors. Yee-hoo!

I knew she'd be mad I didn't have Mr. G. call to confirm, but I'd simply say, that in all my excitement, I'd forgotten. Quite a bit of fibbing was going on, yes, but the way I saw it, the most important things *were* true. I was going to a concert (true), adults would be everywhere, so we wouldn't be downtown alone (true), and I had a ride home (the bus). Did she really need to know the other details?

We spent two hours listening to Madonna songs, getting gussied up, and getting pumped. I thought we looked amazingly foxy in our miniskirts, lace stockings, fingerless gloves, bracelets covering both arms, and nylon bows tied in the center of our wildest hair yet! We even created fake moles above our lips using a single dot of waterproof mascara, guaranteed not to smear. I was jittery, excited, unable to calm down. We were actually going to see the most fantastic woman on the planet perform tonight! We *had* to look our best!

Randi showed me the note she was leaving for Mr. G. "How's this sound?"

Dad,
Change of plans, headed to the concert with Tanya and her mom after all. I'll be home shortly after 11. Love

you!

"Perfect," I said. "He knows where you are and when you'll be home."

But she was a nervous wreck, re-reading the note aloud again and double checking the ringers were turned off. She was freaking me out. She locked the front door behind her and opened the umbrella. "Okay, so he'll come home, see the note, fall asleep in his chair, expect me to wake him up to say goodnight when I get in, and tomorrow I'll turn the ringers back on."

"You don't think Jackie will get any crazy ideas and call the store, do you?" I asked.

"I doubt it. Besides, he'll be teaching till at least 8:30. Rosa will take a message, she won't interrupt class unless it's, like, an emergency."

I spun around. "This is actually going to work! Are we forgetting anything?"

She patted her purse. "Nope, I think we've got everything. Too bad it's so yucky out though. This sucks."

It was true, this weather blew major chunks. Foggy, drizzling, and chilly—the paper said fifty-four degrees would be the high today, and tonight, cool with thunderstorms. But it didn't matter; nothing could get me down today! We shared the only umbrella Randi had, a pink and black, polka dotted one, and boogied down to bus stop.

Randi said, "I've got $24.88, plus $1.25 for the bus. How 'bout choo?"

"I have $23 even, plus this." I pulled out a Ziploc full of wheat pennies and nickels. "Here's $5.18 in change in case we want posters. So, $28.18, minus the $1.25 for bus fare, that's $26.93."

Randi curtsied. "Ye hath a plethora of coin m'dear. No wonder thy purse is insanely heavy," she boomed in some weirdo Shakespearian voice.

"What's a plethora?" I asked, leaping over a small puddle. My shoes were already drenched.

"It's, like, a ton of something," she answered in her regular voice.

"Oh."

While we stood waiting for the bus, we counted five horn beeps, two whistles, and a scream out the window. "Hey, hot stuff!" We giggled every time. We knew we looked totally cute. When the bus finally arrived fifteen minutes late, we thought it was so cool it was packed with girls dressed like us, all headed to the concert. Randi grabbed a schedule from the slot. "Crap, the last bus tonight is at 10:15. On the *weekends* they run until 10:35."

I said, "I'm sure we'll run into some girls from school, we'll catch a ride with one of them."

She nodded.

Had I known the closest stop to the arena was on Smithfield Street, blocks and blocks away, I'd have never worn my denim, baby doll shoes with a slight heel. "I wish I'd worn different shoes," I said, limping a little.

Randi looked down at her black pumps. "Totally. My feet are killing me already. But these shoes go best with this outfit, what could I do?"

I was happy when it stopped raining and we were able to wrap up the umbrella. There were droves of people everywhere, and the closer we got, the more hysterical we became. We were here!

It was mostly girls our age—with friends, not parents—high school girls, littler ones with their moms, and there were even groups of guys dressed in drag wearing makeup, leotards, and fingerless gloves. How cool was that? It felt fantastic to walk among those who shared the same adoration for our beloved pop goddess. These people understood how important this night was. There was no need to explain that here, tonight, we were one. There'd be no "hells bells" reactions to my outfit, gloves, or crucifixes. No eye rolling or mocking names like bimbette, wannabe, or mall hair. No, tonight, we were kindred spirits. I was with my people.

I told Randi, "Look out for anyone holding a ticket sale sign." There were signs everywhere; it was hard to sort through them all: *I Love You, Madonna! Welcome 2 the Burgh! Will You Marry Me??*

She said, "There are so many people! Is it always this crowded or is it just for tonight?"

"I honestly couldn't tell you, this is my first concert. I was here for the circus, like, twice when I was younger, but it was *nothing* like this. This is a sold-out event, though, so..."

We weaved in and out of the crowd, ducking um-
brellas, signs, people letting loose and dancing to
boom boxes. The energy was electric, I loved it!

"Did you know that Madison Square Garden sold
out in a record thirty-four minutes for this tour?" I
asked.

"No way!"

"Yep. Read it yesterday."

Randi looked at her watch. "It's 7:32. We should
walk up the hill more. It might be easier to read the
signs from up there."

"Good idear."

As we marched up the hill—in heels—reading
every sign along the way, the crowd began shrinking
as people entered the arena for the opening acts. I spotted an old man across the street holding a sign that
read "Need Tickets." "Look." I pointed. "Do you think
it means he *needs* tickets or he's asking if others need
them?"

"Randi said, "Punctuation would help."

We ran across the street. Randi asked, "Hey, man,
are you lookin' for tickets?"

The man with the "Where's the Beef?" hat and
shifty eyes looked around. "Are you?"

"Yes!" I blurted. "We're desperate."

Randi poked me with her elbow and gave me a
look. "I wouldn't say *desperate*," she said, playing it
cool. "It's no big whoop. You got 'em or not?"

"Two left. Fifty cash."

"We'll take them!" I said, pulling out my money.

He said, "Each."

"Each! Randi shook her head. "No way, man, you can go lower than that," she said, sounding like she did this all the time. "General seating's only $14.95 retail."

"This ain't retail, doll. Show me the dough."

"Show me the tickets."

He shook his head.

Randi said, "Look, I'm sure there's another guy around here somewhere. Come on, Sandy, we'll go someplace else."

We're using fake names?

We pretended to start to walk away when dude says, "Hold on, doll. Rock bottom, can't go lower than $35. You won't do better wit' the other guys neither."

We still wouldn't have enough.

I pulled out my bag of change, ready to give him the whole thing. "But we only have around $25 each. It's all we have."

"Sorry, kid, find me when ya come up wit' more dough."

Randi said, "All right, thanks."

We walked back down the hill looking for more of those signs. We approached two others, but they were trying to squeeze people for a whopping $65 a pop! And never once did we see them actually holding any tickets. We made our way over to the ticket windows hoping by some miracle there'd be one open, but each one had an "Event Sold Out" sign in it.

"We should just try walking in," I suggested. "What do we have to lose?"

Randi smiled. "Okay."

We tiptoed behind one of the ticket ladies wearing a white shirt and black vest holding a walkie-talkie. She pointed. "Line's over there, ladies."

I smiled sweetly. "Kay, thank you."

So, we stood in line acting as if we truly belonged there, while I drooled over everyone's tickets. They were the most beautiful tickets I'd ever seen. When it was our turn, we tried to mosey past the walkie-talkie lady ripping tickets. She stopped us. "Tickets please."

I laughed nervously. "Oh, I was already inside. I forgot my coat in the car and now I can't seem to find my stub." I gave her a hopeful, cutesy smile and batted my eyelashes.

"Sorry, gotta have your ticket stubs to re-enter."

We nodded and left the line, figuring it was at least worth a try. We walked around checking out all the vendor booths, trying on T-shirts, looking for Ticket-Angels desperate to unload leftovers, but there were none. We found a dry spot beneath the overhang to sit and rest our feet while we ate jumbo pretzels, drank Slurpies, and watched the parking lot grow emptier and emptier by the minute. We could hear a rap group performing and people whistling and cheering.

"I have to pee so bad," I said. "I've been holding it forever."

"Me too. I shouldn't have had that Slurpie, I'm about to burst." She looked around. "They're not going to let us use a restroom without tickets."

I said, "Well, I'm not walking clear down to Burger Barn in these shoes, I'll tell you that." I pointed to a fenced-in area behind the arena where a bunch of tour buses were. "I'm going back there. It's dark now, so no one will see. We'll have to get past them first." I nodded toward the security guys in yellow shirts that said "Staff" on the front.

Randi said, "I'll bet they're guarding the tour buses and side doors." We tiptoed behind the guardrails, looking for an opening in the chain-link fence. We found one where two gates were chained together. There was very little wiggle room, but, luckily, we were both thin enough to squeeze in sideways beneath the chain and padlock. It was much easier than I thought to get back there.

Randi said, "Real fine job the security dudes are doing. What if we were criminals or vandals or something?"

My last week's behavior flashed through my mind. Randi handed me two pretzel napkins she'd hoarded in her purse and took watch while I did my business next to a giant, black bus with tinted windows and tires as big as I was. Then it was my turn to keep watch for Randi. I felt so much better, lighter. Having a full bladder was literally the most annoying feeling in the world but much worse when you were walking in cold, drizzly, weather.

Randi whispered, "I hope we're not peeing by *her* tour bus."

I said, "She wouldn't care, she'd probably do the same thing and wouldn't want two of her biggest fans walking around with uncomfortably full bladders anyway. Do you realize that at this moment she's in *that* building probably doing her makeup and fixing her hair to go on stage?"

"Maybe she's having a snack, you know, for performance energy," Randi said, straightening up her clothes.

Suddenly, a big, burly guy with a walkie-talkie came walking toward us, seemingly from out of nowhere. "Hey, you kids can't be snooping around back here, beat it."

"We know, we know," I said, as we squeezed back out through the fence and began walking toward the entrance.

The light drizzly day had now turned into a full-blown, thunder-stormy night as the two of us stood there under the ledge of the building trying to keep warm. We could hear each song as it came on, and I could tell by the roar of the crowd when Madonna had just done something totally awesome. I felt a pang of envy in my stomach for all the people who were inside getting an eyeful.

By the time the parking lot crews started their garbage cleanup, and food vendors began shutting down, we knew we no longer needed to hold onto our ticket money and decided to each buy two posters and a T-shirt each before we lost the opportunity. We found two milk crates to sit on and crouched under the umbrella, grateful just to be there listening to the songs. Once in a while we could hear her talking to the crowd, and they would go completely wild. Man, I wished we were inside! When "Into the Groove" came on I thought, *so what if it's cold and raining, my feet are killing me, we didn't get tickets, and my hair is a wet mop? We are here and can hear the music, right? Screw this, I'm dancing!*

Randi, who looked tired and bummed out two seconds before, saw me dancing tossed the umbrella to the ground, and jumped up to join me. We twirled around in the rain, singing and laughing. I was genuinely having a blast!

All of a sudden, one of the side arena doors flew open and a young girl who looked to be maybe nine or ten burst out into the rain and puked on the ramp. Ick! She appeared to be all alone, so we ran over to see if she needed some help.

Randi fished some napkins out of her purse and asked, "Are you okay?"

She held her stomach and started bawling as a man rushed out the same door carrying a pink parka, a little purse, bags of cotton candy, and an armful of posters. The girl started throwing up again. She looked like that kid from *The Exorcist*.

"Daddy, I wanna go home," she sobbed.

The man tried calming her down, "Okay, Penny, it's all right." He rubbed her back as she spewed more goo. "That's right... get it all out."

I backed up a few steps, hoping none had splattered on me. It smelled like rotten milk. Randi handed him the napkins. He smiled thankfully as he wiped Penny's mouth and shirt. "She had a little too much cotton candy tonight." He explained. "Mix that with the dancing and being overheated, well..."

I said, "I hope you feel better, Penny. That's happened to me before on Halloween."

"I wanna go home, now, Daddy." She wailed, using her sleeve to wipe her snotty nose.

"I know, let's get you to the car," he said, helping her get into her coat.

Randi said, "Feel better soon!"

"Thanks again for the napkins," he said, as he tossed the bags of candy in the trash can and began walking away.

Then I had an idea. The concert wasn't over yet, and they were *leaving!* "Wait, mister! Sir, I'm so sorry to ask you this, but I have to try. See, we couldn't get tickets and... would it be at all possible for us to snag your stubs?"

He looked confused for a second. "Snag my... oh, yes, ticket stubs." He searched his pockets. "No problem," he said, handing them to me. "Enjoy."

Randi screeched. "Oh, my gawd, sir! Thank you, thank you, thank you so much. You don't know what this means! We hope you feel better, Penny!"

"A thousand thank yous!" I yelled behind me as we booked to the only gate left open.

We ran toward walkie-talkie lady and handed her the stubs. I said, "My friend got sick from a bad pretzel, so we came out for some fresh air, but she feels all better now."

Randi smiled and rubbed her stomach. "Yep, all better. Just needed some cold, rainy air."

The lady eyed our stubs suspiciously. I knew she didn't believe a word we said, but as long as we had those stubs it didn't matter. She looked like she didn't care either way as she stepped aside, and let us push through the metal turnstile. "Y'all better hurry, concert's just about over."

We raced up the ramp and down the first aisle of seats we saw, not having any idea where we were going. I didn't care where the seats were, or about the fact I had to pee again, we were in, baby!

We squeezed our way through crowds of people dancing, laughing, screaming, crying, bouncing balloons back and forth, and holding lighters in the air — it was excitement overload! Blue, pink, purple, and green lights lasered from every direction as jumbo screens located on both sides of the stage showed our shining star shaking a tambourine with two male backup dancers beside her. I screamed my lungs out at the sight of her. I wanted her to know we were there and had come to sing and dance along with her! We held our hands up high and woo-hooed with everything we had! I probably wouldn't have a voice tomorrow, but that was the price you paid for rocking out! The lights dimmed like something was about to happen, then the intro to "Like a Virgin" began. Everyone lost their minds! When it got bright again Madonna was standing at the top of a giant staircase wearing a wedding gown and holding a bouquet with her dancers alongside her. I don't know what in the world came over me—the shock of finally being there, seeing her in the flesh, the energy and emotion of the crowd—but I actually started to cry! I looked over at Randi, and she was crying too. We laughed and wiped our tears.

I pulled my camera out of my purse and snapped a few shots of what I could, but I put it away quickly, I didn't want to miss a moment, we'd already missed so much. The stage was too far away from where we were standing to see small details, but I could see everything great on the Jumbotron. At that moment I realized, every single thing we'd gone through in the past few weeks, all the frustration, was worth every second to be standing right where I was. We let loose, dancing and singing, not caring what we sounded or looked like. It was just like I'd envisioned in my head, except a thousand times better. I could actually feel each beat through my entire body as if we were part of the music, and I wondered if everyone else was feeling that way, too.

After the song, balloons dropped from the ceiling

and the crowd went wild, frantically trying to capture them. Neither of us caught one, but that was okay. She returned to the stage once more for an unforgettable encore and then the concert was over. It didn't matter that we only got to sing along with her and thousands of others for just two and a half songs. They were the *best* songs off the album, if you asked me, and I was more than grateful to have even been there. I still couldn't get over the shock that we'd actually gotten in! And it had all happened so quickly, in the most unexpected way possible. I'd have never guessed, in a million years, it would have transpired that way.

Home or Bust

*R*andi looked at her watch as we charged out the doors. "It's 10:19. If we run, we can still make the bus!"

"Oh! We left the umbrella," I said, as we scrambled down the block as fast as our shoes would allow. The buses seemed to run ten minutes or so behind schedule, so I knew we had a good chance.

Randi said, "Its fine, I'll buy another one."

"But my hair!"

"Tanya, run faster, we have to make it!"

We didn't make it.

At 10:26, we arrived at the stop just in time to see the tail end of our bus round the corner.

I held my side, panting. "Now what?"

Randi pointed down the street to the phone booth

on the corner. "We'll call a cab. We still have enough cash, I'm sure."

"Fine," I said, squeezing my side harder. "But I gotta walk. Cramp."

As we made our way down the block I spotted the sign for Liberty Avenue and laughed. "Oh, my gawd, *this* is Liberty Avenue, and we're walking on it."

"What do you mean?" She asked, attempting to tuck her poster inside her coat.

"Remember what Vera said on Easter? About me looking like a Liberty Avenue streetwalker?"

Randi giggled. "Yep, she sure had you all figured out. This makes it official."

I hesitated as I stood in front of the phone booth with the cracked glass and some kind of food smeared throughout. Chocolate pudding? Fudge? "I do *not* want to go in there, it's beyond disgusting."

Randi nudged the door open with her knee and we squished in, shutting the door behind us.

I covered my nose. "It's like a Petri dish of bacteria in here but at least it's dry."

If I were a hobo, I wondered if I'd be desperate enough to sleep here for the night or if I'd go under a bridge and freeze. It'd be a tough call. I mean, you had to have some standards, even under dire circumstances. I took my mini can of hairspray out and sprayed all around.

"Stop, Tanya! What are you doing? It's not air freshener. You're insane with that stuff!"

"It stinks in here," I whined.

"Well, there's no phone book in here," Randi sighed, sounding annoyed. "How are we supposed to call a cab with no phone book?" She sniffed and looked around. "Do you smell poop?"

I said, "This whole thing smells like an outhouse. Let's just call directory assistance." I tried to remember the name of the cab company that was at my house on Easter. I reluctantly picked up the receiver and that's when I saw it. "Eeeew! Someone smeared poop on the phone!" I shrieked and dropped it as we ran screaming into the rain. I bent down and swished my hand in a pothole puddle, trying not to gag.

We limped three more blocks before finding another pay phone. This one, hanging on the side of a tobacco shop, looked fairly clean except for the graffiti. The artist seemed to really like boobs. I dialed directory assistance.

"City and state please?" The pinched voice asked.

I said, "Pittsburgh, Pennsylvania, I'm looking for a cab company."

"Name?"

"Tanya."

"The name of the cab company is Tanya?"

"I don't know the exact company name. Can you just look up cabs in Pittsburgh and see what name pops up?"

I covered the receiver. "Randi, what's a cab company name."

"I don't know; I never paid attention."

I told the lady. "They're, like, orangish-yellow. I think they have the word yellow in it. Try Yellow's Taxis, please."

I heard the keys clicking rapidly as she searched. "I'm not showing anything under that name."

"Try Yellow's Cabs."

More clicks. "I'm sorry, I'm not seeing any—"

"Tanya, look!" Randi pointed at a bus coming down the street that said, Greentree.

I slammed the phone down and we made a mad dash to the curb, waving our hands wildly. There was no sign or official stop there, so I was ecstatic that he pulled over and let us climb onto the warm, wonderful, *thank God* mobile. We over-thanked him for stopping and tromped all the way to the back. I'd never taken the Greentree before, as it was still quite a distance from where I lived, but I didn't care as long it carried us toward the vicinity of home.

Randi took a schedule from the slot and studied the route. "Looks like it runs along Greentree Road till the very end, and then makes a right into Scott Township, ultimately ending up at Collier Garage."

I took my shoes off and rubbed my toes. "We'll have to get off at the bottom of Greentree Road somewhere before he makes that right turn. If we walk through the shopping center and across the cemetery or Little League fields, we should make it home around the time we said."

"There's no way I'm walking through any cemetery. It'll have to be the baseball park. She checked her watch and smiled. "It's 10:56, we're gonna pull this off."

I closed my eyes, finally able to relax. "Wake me up when we pass the mall." The cozy warmth of the bus was more than I could bear, making it impossible to keep my eyes open. I was wiped out.

I felt the bus pull over to let someone on and when I half opened my heavy lids I saw two of the most gorgeous boys on Earth depositing quarters in the fare box. Randi poked me. I quickly slipped my shoes back on, praying they didn't sit near us. I looked like death warmed over, and even if I'd had enough time to pull out a mirror and fix myself, it wouldn't be enough. I was a bus wreck. They started up the aisle. *Please don't walk back here, please don't.*

They beelined right for the back, just like Randi and I always did, and sat in the seats directly across from us. *Why, oh, why?* They looked about fifteen or sixteen and wore the same uniforms: Black pants with a maroon shirt that had Cinema-City stitched across the front. They wore name tags on the pockets that said, "Hello, I'm Charles" and "Hello, I'm Adam." I was so embarrassed to be seen like this by a regular human, let alone two aces, I didn't make eye contact. I could feel them checking us out though, it was pure torture. My eyes darted everywhere but at them, and when I finally allowed myself to look their way, they were grinning at us. Charles, with the big, brown eyes and dimples, was smiling at me, and his friend, Adam, at Randi. They obviously had to be cuckoo birds to be smiling at us this way, our hair was drenched and we both had eye makeup smeared under our eyes.

Adam broke the awkward silence. "Hey."

Randi said, "Hi."

I raised my hand in a little salute and looked from Charles to Adam. I didn't know which one was cuter, they were both so handsome.

Charles smiled at me. "Do you work on Liberty?"

Ah! "What kind of crack is that?" I fumed.

He looked confused, "At one of the restaurants. You're hostesses, right?"

"Oh, I... I'm sorry." I smiled. "No, we're coming from a concert."

Adam said, "We've never seen you on this route, we just assumed you started training somewhere. They're hiring for the summer at Willy's Seafood Grill and Baggaburgers, in case you're interested."

Randi said, "We missed the South Hills bus."

Adam nodded, "That explains it. So, you go to Seaton High then?"

She said, "Not until August. We're freshman."

Charles said, "I thought for sure you were sophomores. What's your name, blondie?"

"I'm Tanya. This is Randi."

"Everyone calls me Chaz. They make me wear Charles on my tag at work though." He smiled. "It's embarrassing."

Besides his handsomeness, he had a shy, boyish quality I thought was adorable.

Randi asked, "Will you be at Seaton when we get there?"

Adam said, "Don't I wish. No, we go to St. Sebastian Academy."

Beautiful Chaz asked, never taking his eyes off mine, "Do you ever go to Cinema-City?"

I shook my head. "Parkville Theatre."

Adam said, "We work Tuesday and Friday nights, and Sunday afternoons. They give us free passes all the time. Stop by and see us, we'll hook you up."

Randi smiled. "That sounds nice."

I couldn't take my eyes off Chaz's. I wondered what kissing him would be like and felt a hot blush fill my cheeks. "When's your birthday?" I asked.

"October twenty-eighth. Why? Is that when I'll get to take you to a movie?" He came and sat next to me. Adam had already moved next to Randi.

I laughed. "No, I just wanna see what sign you are."

"Oh, yeah, horoscopes. My sister drives me batty with those. When's *your* birthday, Miss Tanya?"

I wished I'd had time to put a piece of gum in my mouth before they'd gotten on and wondered if my breath was okay. I couldn't very well hold my hand up to my mouth and check, could I?

"Mine? November first."

"That would make you a..."

"Scorpio."

"Are two Scorpios compatible?"

I fidgeted with my jacket buttons and said, "I'm not sure, but I'll be sure to look that up."

I could hear Randi and Adam having a conversation about their favorite movies of the year and exchanging numbers. Adam stood up and pushed the signal button for the next stop.

Chaz pulled a work pen and a bus transfer out of his pocket, ripped it in half, and wrote his number down. He handed me the other half and the pen. "I'd love to call you sometime and hear more about the horoscope thing. And maybe see a movie?"

I wrote my number down, trying to make my writing as cute as possible while the bus was bouncing up and down the road. I drew a little heart beside my name. My own heart was literally beating out of my chest. Those few minutes he sat next to me, staring straight into my eyes, made me feel like I'd stopped breathing, and my face felt flushed. I'd never given my number to a boy before.

I handed him the paper and when I tried giving the pen he said, "You keep it. And I'm glad you missed your bus."

They walked to the front as Adam called back, "See you Saturday."

We waved to them from our window as the bus pulled away. Thank goodness we were the only two left because we shrieked like banshees, probably scaring the dickens out of the driver.

Randi said, "We're meeting them Saturday at three for a matinee." She melted in her seat as she put her hands on her cheeks and breathed, "Adam is a total ace! Did you see that smile? He's turning sixteen in September and is getting his driving permit soon."

I sighed. "Did you see the dimples on Chaz? And that name, it's so rad! Randi, this is seriously the most awesome night of my life. The concert, free tickets, and dates this weekend!" I kissed the paper with his phone number on it. "Do you realize it was fate we missed that bus? Wait till we tell the girls, they'll freak!"

Randi looked out the window and pushed the signal button to get off. The moment we stepped into the cold air my nostrils burned. And I hated walking in the cold with a full bladder. At least it wasn't raining anymore, I thought, as we trekked down the hill. "I have to pee," I announced, ducking behind one of the dumpsters of the empty shopping center. "Keep watch."

"Kay, hurry," she said, handing me a napkin.

I laughed. "How many napkins did you swipe for one soft pretzel? You might be some kind of future hoarder." I was one to talk.

"I don't know, ten? You never know when you're gonna need 'em, and they're free. Thanks to my napkin hoarding, you've wiped your butt all night, and little Penny's not wearing puke for makeup. I save people."

I giggled. "You're silly."

After we trudged through the park and Little League fields (all three of them), gushing about the concert and bus ride, we stood there on the road, feet smothered in mud, faced with a choice. We could walk up a giant hill and down the boulevard the right way, on sidewalks, which would add another twenty minutes, minimum, of walking to our already bone tired bodies, or we could slash that time in half by detouring through a few blocks of yards.

I kicked at the curb in an attempt to fling off some of the mud from my shoes. "Well, Dandy-Randi, what do you think? Yards or Boulevard?"

"Seriously, Tanya, I can't... I don't think I can walk that whole boulevard tonight. My feet are in agony."

"I agree. I'm fine with the yards, but it's gonna be dark. No street lights."

"I don't care at this point. It's getting late, and I've gotta get outta these shoes. We just have to be super quiet; someone might think we're cat burglars."

"Cat burglars?" I laughed, tiptoeing between someone's garage and garbage cans. "You've been watching way too many cartoons."

"Shhh. You know what I mean."

I knew it'd be tough to see back in those yards, but it was also foggy, wet, and hilly in some places—the furthest thing from ideal conditions when traveling through unknown territories. But, somehow, we successfully crept through the first section of yards, unseen and unheard, choosing ones without fences for obvious reasons. What I didn't like was how hard it was to tell what I was walking on—mud, grass, mulch, rocks, swampy puddles, garden plots, or manure. All I knew for sure was my feet were now two blocks of mud straight up my ankles. You couldn't even tell I was wearing shoes anymore. As we carefully inched our way down a steep, grassy knoll, I grabbed for any random thing I could for support—pine tree branches, clothes line poles, a miniature, decorative windmill.

"Watch out for the clothes line," I warned. The last thing one of us needed was to get choked.

Randi slipped on the grass and out of pure reflex, grabbed for my left hand, causing me to lose my balance. I yelped as I slid down the hill on my hip bone, taking Randi down with me. She lay on her stomach beside me. My shirt slid up and the left side of my rib cage felt like I'd gone sledding on gravel—my skin, the sled.

"I'm so sorry, Tanya. Are you hurt?"

"Other than being covered in... God only knows what, and scraping my side, I'm fine. You?"

"Help me find my shoe, please."

We crawled around, pawing and patting the sloppy ground, searching for Randi's pump.

"It has to be right here," I said. "We only fell five feet or so."

The next thing I knew, a barking mutt was running straight at us from the next yard over. We scrambled to our feet, sliding everywhere, and ran for the crab apple trees in the back of the yard. I didn't need to look behind me to know it was right at my heels. All I could think of was how many rabies shots we'd need to survive this attack.

With more power than I ever knew I had, I leapt up into the first tree I saw with the lowest, most accessible branches and scaled it in mere seconds. Spiderman would be proud.

"Randi!" I whispered frantically. "Randi, where are you?"

"Here... up here, " she whispered, crouched in the tree next to mine. "Did it get you?"

"No."

We were at least six feet off the ground and safe from the yard yapper. The little jerk paced between the two trees, undecided about which one of us he'd like to gobble up first. He stood on his hind legs and tried hopping up at us. His high pitched, maniacal bark didn't seem particularly vicious, but he *did* mean business. *With a knick-knack paddywhack, give the dog a bone...*

"Shhh. Get! Go away," I whispered.

As the minutes ticked by, for what seemed like forever, I lay my head on the branch as he barked relentlessly. Sometimes he'd mix it up. Growl, bark, whine, yap, growl, cry.

"I wish he'd shut the hell up," Randi said. "We can't sit in this tree all night. And *both* of my shoes are gone."

My ribs were on fire. I pulled up the side of my shirt. "Am I bleeding?"

"I can't see from here, but it looked pretty scraped up from what I could see before demon-dog ran out."

"I guess he thinks we're *cat* burglars." I laughed. "Get it? Cats... up a tree."

"Very funny. Ha ha."

"Do you think he'd bite us if we came down?" I asked. "He's pretty fired up. Maybe if I throw a crab apple, he'll think it's a ball and wanna play."

Yap! Yap! Yap! Yap!

Then it dawned on me, I *knew* what this was! "Do you get what's going on here?"

"Yes, were trapped between the branches of two trees by the tiniest dog alive."

"No. I mean, yeah. But, Randi, this is *our* karma!"

"For *what*? Having a great time?"

"For what? For lying, sneaking out, the broken window, using a puking kid's stubs for our own joy, laughing at Stacy's bald head—all of it."

"You're talkin' kooky. You're reading way too much into it."

Suddenly, a porch light came on two houses down, and a man in a robe opened the screen door. "Rocky! Come 'ere, boy!" He whistled. "Get in here. You leave them 'coons alone."

So, the jerk's name was Rocky.

I prayed we were wearing enough mud to camouflage us in the branches. Rocky didn't know if he should obey his owner or keep yapping at us. He growl-barked in our direction once more before trotting off to the house. Good choice, Rocky. Good boy.

Hallelujah! We waited about a minute after the light went off before we dropped down and took off running—poor Randi without shoes. I'd have offered up one of mine, but she wore a size seven and I was an eight and a half or nine, depending on the shoe.

It was 11:42 by the time we reached my block, and when I got a full view of Randi under the streetlights, shoeless, limping down the sidewalk, covered in mud, I cracked up so hard I choked on my own spit.

Randi, cracking up herself, said, "Tanya, your skirt is literally pulled up to your belly button. You're walking around in your underwear!"

I quickly yanked it down and said, "At least I have shoes!"

"Yeah, that look like they were purchased at Frog Swamps R Us!"

I giggled as I looked down at myself, assessing my own damage. I was also covered in mud, but shocked to see the knuckles on my right hand were scraped and bleeding (from what?), my tights had holes in both knees from scaling the tree, and my left side had one heck of a brush burn. We looked like zombies. Maybe I'd be one for Halloween this year.

Randi sneezed, "I actually have mud in my nostrils."

I said, "Hmm, if only you had a napkin."

"Hmm, wonder where they all went?" She took her glove off and blew her nose in it."

"You're so grody!"

"Ay, I gotta do what I gotta do." She said in a mockingly thick, New York accent.

When we got closer to my house she said, "I won't have a problem sneaking in my side door and jumping in the shower, my dad's probably crashed. But you... how will you explain coming in like this to Jackie?"

And that's when I saw it. That unmistakably familiar, white Caravan parked in front of my driveway, and all the lights in the house were on. "Oh, God."

Randi gasped.

Busted!

"What's my dad doing here? He's supposed to be home sleeping!" Randi paced back and forth, her eyes, wild.

"And *we're* supposed to be at a concert with one of the two of them," I said, sitting down on the cold, concrete porch step. "We're *so* busted."

Randi sighed. "We'd better get in there and face the music before it gets any later. They're probably hysterical by now."

I gave her a weak smile, "We faced the music, that's why we're in this mess."

Randi said, "Boy, you're on a roll tonight aren't cha."

"Wait, let's go in with positivity," I said. "Not *too* happy, but not all bummed out either. When they see us all discombobulated like this, they'll be like, oh, see? This is why we wanted you to go with an adult. Downtown's dangerous at night."

Randi nodded, straightening her clothes.

"Remember, positivity is catching. Now smile."

We tried fixing ourselves as best we could, walking up the steps, fluffing our matted hair, dabbing at our mascara-streaked, raccoon eyes, and using our sleeves and some spit to wipe mud from our cheeks but only making it worse.

I took a deep breath and opened the door. I poked my head in first so as not to shock her with my appearance. "Heya, Mom, I'm home." I sang, like everything was normal. Mr. G. and Mom were in the dining room. Mom was on the telephone. "Okay, Trish, she's here. Yes, I will. She just walked in. I'll call you in a bit. Mmm-hmm, bye."

When we walked in, the two of them gasped. Mom rushed toward us. "Oh, dear heaven, what happened? Are you all right?" She hugged me, looking more upset than I'd ever seen her. It stabbed at my heart instantly, knowing I was the cause.

"Oh, it looks much worse than it is, Mom, seriously. We got caught in the rain, that's all."

"But you're covered in mud!" Her voice was a little too high pitched.

Mr. G. said, "We've been worried sick about you girls. We didn't know if we should wait for you to call or go looking for you." He looked upset, but relieved.

"Dad, we're fine. I slid down a hill, and Tanya fell trying to help me. What are you doing here?"

My mom held up my note and flicked it. "When I saw this, I had the feeling a visit to the store was *long* overdue. We tried to catch up with you two at Randi's, but you'd already gone." Then she held up Randi's note.

Randi and I looked at each other.

"You deliberately defied me, Tanya!"

I braced myself, ready to take my verbal lumps. I deserved it, I knew.

She pulled out my yellow suspension paper. *Watch me pull a rabbit outta m' hat... ta da!* "And you're *smoking*? Suspended from school? Do I even know you right now?"

Boy, when it rained it poured. How could I defend myself when she was armed to the max with evidence? Freakin' attorneys. This was getting way serious.

"You went rooting around through my stuff?"

"Yes, Tanya, I went into your room *after* I found your note, and this was sticking out of the science book on your desk. See, there's little thing called trust. I *trust* you won't lie to my face, scheme, manipulate, and forge my signature." It sounded way worse when she put it that way. "And with trust, I wouldn't have to 'root around through your stuff.' Trust is a two-way street and the hardest thing to rebuild once it's broken."

Randi, who looked like she was about to topple

over, sat down on the floor. Her dad stood there not knowing what to say about this very personal argument between my mom and me.

With all the sincerity I could muster I said, "Mom, I swear to you I wasn't smoking. I don't smoke, you have to believe me. I was afraid if I told you about the suspension you'd say no to the concert. I was going to tell you about it tomorrow, honest. I embellished—"

"Lied." Mom interrupted.

"Fibbed."

"I'm not going to play semantics with you, Tanya." She crossed her arms, looking intense. I felt sorry for the people that had to see this face in the courtroom. I didn't know what semantics were, but it was clear she didn't want to play them.

"All right, I *lied* on the note, but this wasn't planned for days or anything like that. I don't know. I guess I just thought, what harm would it do? We went to a concert and lied about having a parent with us. We didn't rob a bank or skip town or do drugs or drink alcohol. We ate a pretzel and bought a poster! You *can* trust me, Mom. I screwed up, I know that, but have I ever done anything like this before? No."

She stared through me, her penetrating eyes narrowing in her unwavering search for truth. "Not that I know of; makes me wonder what else I've missed."

"Nothing, Mom, I promise."

Mr. G. sat on the couch. "We know you're both good kids, that isn't the issue. This world can be a dangerous place, and as your parents, we're responsible for keeping you as safe as we can. And if we specifically tell you *not* to do something, *that's* what we mean. You may not always like the boundaries we've put in place or think they're fair, but like it or not, they're there for a reason." He looked at Randi sternly.

She put her head down. "I'm sorry, Dad. We'll never to do anything like that again. And I promise you, Jackie, cross my heart, Tanya was *not* smoking. She just happened to be in the wrong place at the wrong time."

Mom's face softened. "I believe that, Randi, I do. But you forged my signature, Tanya. There could be serious consequences to something like that. Don't you *ever* do that again. Are we clear?"

I nodded. "I'm sorry."

"We're glad you're both home safely." She began switching off some of the lights. "It's late. You're both severely in need of showers."

"Mom, you do believe me about the smoking, don't you?"

She nodded. "Tomorrow I want to hear exactly what occurred. As for tonight's actions, there will be accountability."

Whatever it was, no matter how crappy, I knew I deserved it.

She thought about it a moment. "All right, three weeks grounded. No mall, no movies, no telephone, no allowance."

"Three weeks! That's the middle of June!"

Mr. G. said, "Same goes for you, too."

We both nodded. What choice did we have but to accept it? We'd messed up. That meant no movie this weekend with Adam and Chaz. My first real date with a bodacious hunk and I was grounded! *Karma.*

I grabbed my purse, jacket, and muddy poster. "Since it's a quarter to one in the morning, can Randi just shower and sleep here tonight?"

Mom looked at Mr. G. "That doesn't sound like a bad idea, Joe. Maybe they should stay home from school tomorrow, they're exhausted."

He nodded. "It's been a long night for all of us."

While Mom and Mr. G. walked into the dining room for his keys and coat, Randi and I smiled at each other. That wasn't so bad.

I heard Mom say, "I'm sorry we had to meet under these circumstances. Thank you again for the flowers, they're exquisite."

"It was my pleasure. I'm glad you liked them. And that food you sent over on Easter was... you're quite a chef."

She laughed in a low, throaty way I'd never heard before. "You have such a special way of arranging the bouquets that really accentuates the color of each flower; truly a work of art."

What?

He smoothed his hair back, looking like he was about to say something but couldn't find the words.

I looked at Randi, and she was grinning.

Mr. G. said, "You see, I believe that each plant is unique and—" He smiled. "I'm sorry, it's late."

"No, go on. Your passion for ecology is refreshing."

I couldn't believe these two. They were flirting!

He laughed nervously, "Would you like to grab a cup of coffee sometime?"

Mom tilted her head. "How about now? T's Diner is open twenty-four hours."

He quickly grabbed his coat. "If you like fruit, they make a wonderful, homemade strawberry pie."

Did she like fruit? The woman was obsessed with it. She wore it as perfume for Pete's sake!

They came into the living room as Mom, in her usual fashion, tried to locate where she'd last seen her purse. "Girls, we're heading out for coffee (she hated coffee). We won't be long." She gave us both hugs. "Get your showers and get under some warm blankets. Let's put this day behind us."

"We are sorry, Mom... Mr. G. You don't have to worry about us doing anything like this again. Trust me, we learned our lesson."

They nodded.

"Randi, I want you to call me when you get up." Mr. G. said, holding Mom's coat for her as she wiggled into it and smiled at him. "Get some sleep, girls."

I nodded, suddenly remembering that dream I had with all the flowers everywhere and him barbecuing, and a weird déjà vu feeling came and went. Randi and I hurried over to the window to watch them leave. Mom threw her head back and laughed at something he said as he held her door open like a gentleman. We giggled deliriously. What a night!

Fate

*a*fter concert-gate, as Mom playfully called that night, our lives changed dramatically. We stayed grounded for about two weeks before we were let off the hook for good behavior. The first week of June, Randi and I graduated from the eighth grade and could now officially call ourselves high school girls!

Randi had snuck in a call to Adam to let him know we weren't standing them up, we'd simply be "tied up" for a few weeks. When we were done with our sentence we did meet them for a movie, where Chaz held my hand, and we talked a few times on the phone. But his family was flying to Greece for a couple weeks to visit his grandparents and wouldn't be back until the middle of July when I'd be at camp. We promised to keep in touch, and I wrote about him in my journal almost every day.

Randi and I bought pool passes and spent every day there from noon until till six, working on our tans, reading magazines, gorging on licorice. We came up with a secret tanning oil formula to get us darker faster, consisting of baby oil, iodine, blended cherries, and watermelon juice. We had to stop using it once the bees started chasing us. We just knew one of our recipes would stick one day and we'd become the famous mixologists we were meant to be.

The pool was the perfect place to start the summer off before leaving for camp. When it wasn't too busy we'd play Marco Polo with some of the cooler lifeguards, and Randi had a major crush on a junior guard named Eric, who she *never* stopped blabbing about. He definitely liked her too, because every chance he got he'd swim over to the wall and splash water on her feet while she was tanning. She'd jump up and pretend to be mad and call him a booger or a toad, and he'd swear it was an accident. They were ridiculously cute. Randi said as soon as she turned fifteen she was signing up for the junior guard program.

Aside from a few cute lifeguards, I didn't think there were many crush-worthy boys there. The one I liked was in Greece and my other crush, Jay Garrick, was practicing baseball on the lower field during the day and playing games at night.

Randi's dad, Joe, he insisted I call him, was obsessed with the game. It was Mets this, and Yankees that. The man was like a walking trivia card, too. There wasn't anything he didn't know about the sport—players stats, team overall wins in 1962. You couldn't stump him, he was inhuman.

He took the four of us to a few games and bought us hats and giant foam fingers to wave around. It was the first time I'd ever been to a baseball game, and I loved it—there were hunks everywhere!

Randi and I had officially become what Aunt Trish called boy crazy. Boys were *all* we talked about anymore. It was as if our movie date and hand holding had opened some kind of floodgate. At the games, we'd leave Mom and Joe and find two empty seats by ourselves and snack on Cracker Jacks, rate the players by cuteness, and really get into chanting, "Let's go, Bucs! Let's go, Bucs!" And sometimes, depending on whether they won or not, there were fireworks.

Speaking of fireworks...

After "concert-gate", Jackie and Joe spent a lot of time having coffee. Saturday mornings Mom would get up early and help him at the store, or I'd wake up and see them out back digging around the garden. Then they'd head off to the farmer's market. And all of this before I'd even gotten out of bed!

The second week of July, Randi and I left for summer arts camp. But before we did, the lovebirds, as we called them, had already gone to several movies, a bookstore poetry reading, a folk concert, and one night they'd gotten all snazzied up to meet Aunt Trish and her boyfriend at the ballet.

We were away at camp for Mom's birthday, but when we got home, she told us how Joe surprised her with a romantic weekend getaway to see one of their favorite hippie bands somewhere. Yep, those two were like two peas in a pod, peanut butter and jelly, salt and pepper, pork and beans... you get the picture. I'd never seen my mother happier. It was truly a magical, unforgettable summer for all of us.

Soon, the hot days turned cool, and it was back-to-school time. Ninth grade was everything we expected and more, but that's another story.

That fall, Randi and I both turned fourteen and signed up for babysitting jobs in the community registry. We worked two nights a week for a few hours, plus, we still received allowances, so we were raking in the bucks, which we spent mostly on concert tickets and clothes. Not the kind we used to wear either. It seemed we'd grown into a very different phase of fashion and music. In August we went to see Amy Grant and Tina Turner live, which was unbelievable! We were picked up and dropped off, of course. In September, we saw Cheap Trick, November, Hall & Oates, and we were already saving for Aerosmith, in March. We were becoming quite the concert connoisseurs and bought a T-shirt from each show.

Since we both tried out and made the Seaton High Dance Team, had babysitting jobs, and school work, that didn't leave much time to hang out with Stacy and Paula. We were all still friendly and hung out in the bathroom and at lunch but shared barely any classes, only health and gym. And believe it or not, Stacy joined the drama club, and Paula was a cheerleader! Things sure can change a lot in a year.

In November, the love birds drove us seven hours to New Jersey to spend Thanksgiving with Randi's, hysterically entertaining, Italian *famiglia*. They were thunderous, lovable, and straight up. You never had to guess what they were thinking or feeling. Two long tables were pushed together, and there was a smaller table on the end of that for the kids.

Halfway through dinner Joe stood up and clinked his glass with a fork. "Everyone, I have an announcement." Randi and I gave each other a knowing look.

"As you all know, I've met a special woman and her equally wonderful daughter." Everyone sat on pins and needles. "These past six months have been the happiest of my life." He looked like he was about to cry. He raised his glass to me and Randi. "I want to thank you girls, whose friendship introduced me to my soul mate. I can't see spending one day of my life without her." He reached for Mom's hand. "I've asked her to marry me."

The entire room held their breath.

"And I said yes!" she screamed.

Randi's aunts flew from their seats and squeezed my mom, then me, then Randi, then Mom again. I couldn't understand a word they were saying in Italian but there were tears of joy.

Randi and I sat there smiling with tears in our eyes. We'd literally seen this coming from the moment he'd asked her to coffee. I sensed something was up by the goofy way they'd acted after their dinner date last night, and by how teary-eyed Mom acted all day, saying how much she loved me. We clinked apple juice and wine glasses and cheered as the adults rambled on about soul mates and family.

Joe said, "More than anything we want you girls to be happy."

Randi said, "We are, Dad."

I nodded. "We couldn't be happier about this." And I meant it. I positively adored my soon-to-be dad and sister. I was going to have a family. We'd be just like a real-life Brady Bunch!

My mom sniffled. "Sometimes it takes a lifetime to find the right one." They looked into each other's eyes and everyone sighed.

Joe kissed her hand. "When you know, you know, right?"

Those two were on a real trip to la la land.

Aunt Rose raised her glass. *"Applausi al destino!"*

(Cheers to fate!) Everyone cheered.

Joe laughed. "Did we tell you the story of how we met?"

Everyone laughed as Mom and Joe retold the story of how we'd snuck out for a concert and left them notes, not thinking they'd cross paths, and that we'd walked in soaked and covered in mud. It really was hilarious the way they told it.

Joe said, "At the risk of sounding corny, it really was love at first sight."

She hugged him and smiled. "For me too."

"When's the big day?" Randi asked.

Joe said, "Well, we wanted to marry on the anniversary of the day we met, May 28th, but then we thought, why wait? So, we're planning it for March, for Easter break. You'll have the time off from school to travel."

"Travel?" Randi asked.

Mom said, "We wanted to have our wedding and honeymoon together as a family, to marry on the beach at sunset."

"The beach?" I asked.

She and Joe exchanged looks. Mom said, "That's right, the four of us are going to Hawaii for spring break!"

Randi and I jumped up from the table so fast our chairs flew over backwards. We bounced up and down screaming, "Hawaii! Oh, my gawd! Hawaii!"

Randi screamed, "We're gonna be *so* tanned!"

"That's just four months away!" I yelled at the top of my lungs, suddenly aware of the fact I was doing that at the dinner table. And you know what? No one cared! They were all talking and laughing and yelling over each other themselves. It was pretty awesome to be in a house where expressing yourself and letting loose a bit was encouraged.

There was no one staring me down, calling me a heathen or a floozy, or making fun of my big hair. As a matter of fact, all of Randi's aunts had big hair, long nails, and wore more makeup than I'd ever seen. They were glamorous, Italian women who looked like they'd stepped straight out of a salon.

Joe said, "Of course, whoever wants to join us is more than welcome. Jackie's best friend, Trish, has generously arranged a forty percent discount on your flights, and I've already rented a house for that week, right on the beach, with plenty of room for all of you."

Everyone at the table went totally bonkers. None of this seemed real. Hawaii! What would I wear? What would I take? I'd never even been on an airplane before. Randi and I already felt like sisters, so it was cool they were getting hitched and all, but a trip to Hawaii for spring break? Now *that* was a wedding!

I sat back in my chair and watched everyone around me eating, passing bowls, laughing, and "busting each other's balls" as Uncle Rudy said. They'd already made me feel like one of their own, with their approving smiles, kisses, hugs, cheek squeezes, and hair and makeup tips. It truly felt like home. I couldn't wait until the wedding, to have Randi as a sister and Joe as my dad, to be part of this wonderful family. The Gattano family.

And that's how it happened. How one night changed my entire life; how our parents fell in love at first sight, and my best friend in the whole world became my sister, and how I finally had the kind of big family I'd always dreamed of.

And now that I understand more about fate, destiny, serendipity, and good old-fashioned luck—how one chance meeting or moment could change *everything*—I couldn't wait to see what happened next.

Acknowledgments

Judith G., my dearest friend and confidante, thank you for your encouragement, expert advice, and mentorship. My husband, Jason, I'm truly grateful for your never-ending support and optimism. David M., beta reader extraordinaire, BFF, and huge supporter, thank you for your friendship and for always being there. Special shout out to Sergio, the *best* stylist in the "Burgh." Thanks for the hilariously nostalgic trips down 80s lane.

About the Author

KRISTY JO VOLCHKO is the author of the children's adventure series Cackleberry Creek, which includes such titles as, *Frogs Can Fly*, *There Are No Monsters at Cackleberry Creek*, *The Clubhouse Cabobble*, and *Operation Scrub-A-Dub Skunk*.

A multi-genre author and blogger, she began writing stories as young as eight years old and has since penned numerous books, short stories, and poetry anthologies that have become popular around the globe. Kristy lives in Pittsburgh, Pennsylvania, where she continues to share her love of storytelling.